LAW OF THE WEST

Coldiron reached out and his fingers brushed the cool softness of Susan Penfold's cheek.

She stepped back from him. "Why did you do that?"

"It seemed the right thing to do and I wanted to," Coldiron replied.

"My husband has been dead hardly a week."

"Feelings are important, not time or custom," Coldiron said.

"They are important to me," said Susan.

"We're not in Massachusetts. We're in the Colorado Territory searching for two men to kill. Does that sound like Massachusetts? There, the law would be doing the looking, and if the outlaws were caught, a trial would be held. Here, if we catch them, we will kill them. Or they will kill us. . . ."

SHADOW OF
THE WOLF

SHADOW OF THE WOLF

F. M. PARKER

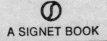

A SIGNET BOOK

NEW AMERICAN LIBRARY

PUBLISHER'S NOTE

This novel is a work of fiction. Names, characters, places, and incidents either are the product of the author's imagination or are used fictitiously, and any resemblance to actual persons, living or dead, events, or locales is entirely coincidental.

This is an authorized reprint of a hardcover edition published by Doubleday & Company, Inc.

 SIGNET TRADEMARK REG. U.S. PAT. OFF. AND FOREIGN COUNTRIES
REGISTERED TRADEMARK—MARCA REGISTRADA
HECHO EN CHICAGO. U.S.A.

SIGNET, SIGNET CLASSIC, MENTOR, ONYX, PLUME, MERIDIAN and NAL BOOKS are published by New American Library,
1633 Broadway, New York, New York 10019

First Signet Printing, October, 1986

1 2 3 4 5 6 7 8 9

PRINTED IN THE UNITED STATES OF AMERICA

THE MOUNTAINS—
A PROLOGUE

The unnamed mountains were ancient beyond imagination. They had been formed during an era tens of millions of years before man came into being. An immense force had compressed and arched the rock mantle of the earth, bending and thrusting the thick layers of stone miles upward. Crumpled and broken, the jagged spires pierced deeply into the blue sky.

Along fractured and shattered zones in the folded rocks, mineral-rich fluids percolated upward. As the solutions migrated through different temperatures and pressures, various elements precipitated out. One was a malleable, yellow metal. It was deposited in pods and stringers and formed hidden lodes that contained thousands of pounds of the substance.

Rivulets, creeks and rivers relentlessly scoured and wore away the mountains. A few cut into some of the rich concentrations of the heavy metal. The water tumbled the golden crystals downstream, pounding and deforming them into irregular, rounded nuggets, to finally drop them in gravel bars and crevices in the bedrock.

In a span of time that was only one tick in the life clock of the mountains, the world turned cold and glaciers grew on the high, frigid crowns and coves and flowed down to fill the valleys. A great continental glacier more than a mile thick crunched a devastating swath in from the northeast, to halt only a short distance from the mountains.

Mighty animals, the woolly mammoth, the saber-toothed

tiger and the giant condor thrived in this land of violent arctic storms. Then time whispered once again and in only a few thousand years the glaciers retreated like the surf of a white, viscous ocean and vanished. So too, gone forever, were the magnificent giant animals of that epoch.

The soft tread of moccasined feet soon sounded upon the mountain as a race of copper-skinned men pushed their dauntless way from the northwest. And the herds of buffalo that had fled before the killer glaciers, now returned, winding their course, following the appearance of the grass upon a land that had not known its greenness for millennia.

The humans divided into clans and drifted apart, spreading across the high country and the plains that lay to the east. The expanse of land was so broad that the tribes were separated for generations, so long a time that the language they spoke became unalike and they could not converse. Thus, they became strangers, and therefore enemies, who fought and slew each other and stole each other's women.

For the very first time the mountains received a name. The brown men called them the Shining Mountains, for in the evening when the falling sun settled upon the tall peaks, they began to glow with a brilliant light as if consuming themselves to hold back the black night just a little longer.

The copper-colored man found the golden nuggets in the creek bottoms and crystals of it in stringers slicing through the quartz rocks of the steep mountain slopes. Sometimes he would hammer the strange rock that would bend and change shape under hard blows, but not break like other rocks. Then, his curiosity satisfied, he selected the truly hard stone, the quartz which would fracture in a skilled hand into long, thin cutting blades.

Sharp points and edges killed game and enemies. Who could have use for a soft rock?

A few thousand years passed and a strange new species of animal appeared. It was a stalwart brute, long legged and wiry, and could run like the spring wind. This new beast, called *mustaño* or cayuse and a dozen other names, increased prodigiously and quickly spread throughout the mountain valleys and the plains. Upon the whole land, only one other species of animal, the buffalo, could compete with him for the life-sustaining grass.

A second race of man arrived, crossing the wide eastern plains and climbing up into the mountains. It was a white breed, warlike and possessive. Looking about, he saw not the mountains shining; instead, he saw sky-high stone ramparts impossible to cross, loose talus slopes perched dangerously steep against them, and the valleys choked with boulders.

He renamed the mountains. The Rockies.

The white man found the golden stones. His numbers multiplied prodigiously as thousands of his kind swarmed to the discovery, forcing their way up the canyons, scaling the perilous ramparts and tearing the metal from its resting place.

This white breed drove the brown man from the mountains. The brown man retreated onto the great flat plains that contained no gold. Where one of his villages once sat upon the banks of a stream at the foot of the mountains, a new and different town sprang up.

A town of white men. Called Denver.

CHAPTER 1

Gachupin Basin, Colorado Territory, March 5, 1864.

In the rimrocked mountain valley, the bony roan stallion stood on trembling legs and rested his weary head upon the top of the ice and snow wall. He looked with starving eyes at the tufts of grass sticking up above the snow only a scant few yards outside his reach.

Seventeen mares lay dying upon the hard-packed snow behind the stallion. The ribs and backbones of their famished bodies showed painfully sharp through their hides. Nothing about them moved except the shallow expansion of their lungs as they breathed.

Beyond the giant snowdrift that penned in the stallion and his mares, other bands of horses pawed in the snow and then lowered their heads to feed upon the life-giving grass they had uncovered. The roan stud remembered how sweet the wild mountain grass was. He pushed feebly at the white barrier, trying to go join the free ones.

For the thousandth time, the stallion surrendered to the impassable barricade. Then, still gazing off across the basin, he slowly started to lick the ice with his parched tongue.

At the extreme limits of his vision, where the rimrocks of the valley had been cut apart by the creek, three dark forms came into sight.

The two riders hurried their long-legged horses through the knee-deep snow blanketing the bottom of the narrow canyon.

Clifford Yerrington led, impatiently casting anxious glances ahead into Gachupin Basin. Luke Coldiron trailed close behind, towing a packhorse.

Overhead, low dark clouds, their snow-swollen bottoms brushing the tops of the canyon rims, scudded to the southeast on the bite of the freezing wind. Four ravens, seeking shelter in the brushy crown of a large pine tree, took alarm at the passage of the men. Cawing loudly to each other and pumping powerfully with broad black wings, they launched themselves from their perch and kited away, riding the turbulence of the invisible river of air.

Luke looked ahead at his gray-headed old comrade hunched up in a sheepskin coat with a felt hat pulled down low to rest on the tops of his ears. "Ease up, Cliff. We're almost there," Luke called.

Cliff turned, and the wind wrenched loose a strand of his long white hair, and it flicked and danced about his face. His dark brown eyes examined Coldiron.

"You are right. We have reached the valley. I hope we are in time to correct whatever is wrong."

"You could be mistaken about your feelings. Everything might be all right."

"It would please me if things were safe and this long ride has truly been for nothing," said Cliff. "Thanks for going along with my premonition. But that nagging feeling in my head that I must get back to the ranch was just too strong to ignore."

Luke nodded his understanding. The two of them had left the ranch in early December and had ridden to Santa Fe. They had planned to spend the cold months toasting before a warm fire in the elegant La Fonda Hotel and to enjoy the companionship of many friends. In the spring when the snow melted in the mountains, they would return to the high-country ranch.

On the first day of March Cliff began to pace the floor worriedly. He told Luke they should go at once to the ranch. There was trouble there. On the second day Luke surrendered to Cliff's prodding, for the old man's forebodings in the past had often proven correct.

They had crossed the mighty Sangre de Cristo Mountains along the snow-filled valley of the Rio Fernando de Taos.

Then onward, forcing a way through the gorge of the Cimarron River. They turned north to climb toward the headwaters of the Vermejo River and Gachupin Basin high on the flank of the Culebra Mountains. The ninety miles of steep, snowy trails had been traveled in three days.

Cliff pulled rein at a tall slabstone fence blocking entry into the basin. He hastily stepped down from his cayuse and with a quick sweep of his arm, brushed the snow from the top of the wall. He hoisted himself up on it. Luke also mounted the stone fence and from that height scanned the frozen and windswept terrain spread before them.

Luke knew this piece of land like no other upon the whole earth. The valley was long, somewhat oval, and hemmed in on all sides with brown sandstone ledges tens of feet high. The bottom was flat and stretched to the north thirty miles, so far that one end could not be seen from the opposite. The greatest width was three miles across. A few small hills capped with pine were scattered randomly about. Cottonwoods and willows marked the long, looping meanders of a creek running the full north-to-south length of the valley.

He had discovered the valley twenty-one years before while transporting his catch of beaver pelts from the towering Culebras to Santa Fe. More than a thousand wild horses had been grazing the meadows, far more than the land could feed. Many were thin and stunted. He found scores upon scores of skeletons and decaying carcasses of horses that had died of starvation during the winter. Yet Luke had recognized the huge potential of the mountain valley to produce excellent horses.

A month later he returned from Sante Fe with two packhorses straining under heavy burdens of powder and shot. During that first summer he slew more than eight hundred horses, those that were sick, lame, or had poor body form, and most of the stallions. So many animals were slain that the coyotes and wolves stopped hunting, merely following the killer human and growing fat eating the choicest tidbits from the carcasses left at his ambushes.

Out of all that great herd he allowed only two hundred mustangs to live. They became the nucleus from which he now bred the best horses in all the New Mexico and Colorado territories.

Ten bands of horses, their dark bodies etched, sharp and distinct, against the white snow, were within range of his sight. The animals in the nearest group had their heads lifted and closely watched the new arrivals to the basin. A band of six elk on the right at the base of the rimrock began to trot to the north, away from the intruders.

"Everything looks okay at this end of the valley," said Luke.

"Appears that way all right," agreed Cliff. "Can't see the ranch house from here because of the hill blocking that direction."

He clambered down to the ground and regarded Luke. "There's something still in my head telling me to go on."

Without waiting for an answer, Cliff began throwing aside the stones of a section of the fence. Luke joined the old man in the task. Without being too obvious, he lifted the larger slabs, for the strength of his aged friend was failing and his health was frail.

Cliff noticed that Luke was doing the heavier work. He sighed silently to himself. That was like Luke.

He knew he owed Luke his life. Eleven years earlier Luke had found him unconscious in the dirt of San Francisco Street in Santa Fe, an educated gentleman turned gunfighter and gambler and then finally to sink to the lowest status—a penniless drunkard.

Clifford Yerrington had come to consciousness, surfacing up through the alcoholic vapors that numbed his brain, to find a man slapping his face. With his head ringing from the harsh blows, Cliff cursed the man and told him to stop or he would shoot him. The man bent down and shouted one question: "Can you cook?"

"Best of all cooks," Cliff had mumbled in response. So Luke had hoisted him upon a horse, tied him so that he could not fall off and in two days took him to his ranch in this beautiful valley. Cliff had never once thought of leaving.

The gap in the fence was finished, the horses led through and the stones relaid. The two men swung astride and continued north.

"The horses seem to be wintering well," observed Cliff, motioning a hand at the band they were passing.

"Yes, they are," said Luke. "The snow's not so deep but

what they can't dig down to feed.'' He pointed to the left. "I see a mighty big snowdrift off there at the bottom of those ledges. Some mustangs might have got trapped behind it. I've seen it happen before. Let's put on our snowshoes and go take a look.''

They untied the webbed footgear from the back of the packhorse and mushed up the slope of the snowbank. The drift ended abruptly in a six-foot drop. The vertical face was sheeted with ice, shiny and slick.

"Damnation! Look at those poor ponies,'' exclaimed Cliff, staring down from the top of the ice wall at the horses sprawled on the packed snow. They are almost starved to death. Looks like the colts are already dead.''

"They've eaten the limbs of that pine tree until the stubs are half as thick as my wrist,'' said Luke.

At the sound of the voices the roan stallion struggled weakly to his feet and eyed the men. He nickered plaintively. Part of the mares managed to rise, while the rest merely raised their heads and stared at the men.

Luke evaluated the giant snowdrift and the perpendicular face on the horses' side. Where the horses' heads had rested on top, a hard shelf of ice eighteen inches or so wide had been formed. The chest of every animal was without hair, rubbed raw and bleeding. He swung his sight from the horses up to the rimrock.

In his mind's eye Luke could see the roan stud, wise in the ways of mountain winters, guiding his band into the shelter under the ledge to escape the snowstorm. The stallion had not known that above him the top of the rimrock was barren of trees and brush. With nothing to hold the falling snow in place, the gale winds had whipped it up and poured it like a river down into the basin.

The tide of frozen water had added its great volume to that falling naturally onto the lower land. Parallel to the rimrock a monster drift grew, measuring nearly a quarter mile long and a hundred yards wide. Silently and swiftly, the trap had closed upon the stallion and his band.

Luke examined the ice wall and the snow, packed like white stone on the ground. The stud and the mares must have attacked the entrapping mass hundreds of times. They had compacted each ten inches of snow into one inch of ice, winning the fight until the mound of yielding crystals was head high and beyond the reach of their hooves.

The remaining bulk of the snow was compressed into an ice wall by the ramming chests. An unmovable prison wall extended the full length of the drift. The desperate struggle to reach food had failed.

"Cliff, you go on up along the drift and see if any more horses are up there. I'll get the ax from the pack and chop and stomp this snow down until we can get these ponies out."

"Right," said Cliff, and trailing his rifle in his hand, went off along the lip of the snowbank in a rolling, spraddle-legged step to keep his bear-paws from striking each other.

The ice splintered and sailed away under the bite of the sharp ax blade. A sloping ramp began to take form under Luke's blows and tramping feet.

The group of four horsemen, heavily armed with rifles and six-guns and leading two loaded packhorses, moved like silent shadows through the snow of the pine forest. Their mounts were tired, for they had come swiftly the long distance from Denver City. To ease the laborious task of breaking trail, each man followed precisely the tracks made by the horse in front.

The gang stayed concealed in the woods. Now and then on the right the trees thinned and the sandstone ledges rimming Gachupin Basin were visible.

Schiller led, his tall, gaunt body erect and his crafty eyes sweeping the forest all around. The deep snow worried him. It was not possible to move without leaving sign, and a man on horseback could be seen for miles. Poor conditions for what he planned to do.

The skill of the members of his gang would partly compensate for the snow. Tilston, riding directly behind him, was very fast with a gun and always stood firm in the toughest of fights. The two Dragus brothers were sly hombres, back shooters who always found a way to kill any man that threatened them. The three men were the best horse thieves in all the Colorado Territory.

Schiller slowed and turned right toward the rimrock. Slipping his horse cautiously among the black trunks of the trees, he came to the edge of the ledges overlooking the basin. The rest of the outlaw crew crowded near to look.

"I see the ranch house, corrals and bar," said Schiller. He pointed down at an angle at the structures. "If my eyes ain't failed me, there's not one man or horse track anywhere inside the fence surrounding the headquarters. No one is here."

"Our luck may be good," said Tilston. "This may be easier than we thought. From just this one point I can see a dozen bands of mustangs. Should be no big chore to round them up in this snow, since they can't run far in it."

From a distance two clear, sharp rifle shots came speeding swiftly through the cold, heavy air. All the men sighted in the direction of the sound.

Oscar Dragus, the older brother, snorted loudly. "Your luck ain't worth a mule's fart, Tilston. I bet that was Coldiron firing his gun in practice to get ready for us." He spoke to Schiller. "I'm damn near froze. We've come more than two hundred miles through ass-deep snow. What's next?"

Schiller swung a hard eye upon Oscar. "First, you listen to what I've got to say. I'm going to tell you what kind of a hombre this Coldiron is. Over the past twenty years this man has built the biggest horse ranch in this part of the country. He raises the best horseflesh for five hundred miles in any direction. Look down there. He's got one hundred thousand acres of prime meadowland.

"He's known in Santa Fe and Denver City as a tough gent. Some folks call him Old Horse Killer from the way he thinned out those first wild bands of mustangs to get the kind of stock he wanted."

"So he's a hard worker and maybe a little rough. Ain't we still going to take his horses?" asked Oscar sharply.

"Why hasn't some Indian lifted his hair and run off his animals?" questioned Vern Dragus.

"Now that gets closer to what kind of man Coldiron is," responded the gang leader. "He made his own private treaty with Big Tree, chief of the Ute that claim this land. Each year the chief comes here with some of his braves and they take what they think are the best one hundred cayuses from the herd. In turn, Coldiron goes about his business of raising horses.

"Now hear me plain. This man will be hard to kill, and I

don't want any mistakes made. We're not the first men that's come here to take his horses. Just a year ago a band of Mexicans raided him and tore off for Mexico with near three hundred head. Well, he trailed them south for days and right on across the Mex border. He caught up with them and shot the hell out of several. Took the gold they had got for the horses and came home without a scratch. He's not going to be easy like some storekeeper.''

"No man is so tough but what he can't be gunned down,'' growled Oscar. "But if you are afraid of him, why don't we simply bushwhack him?''

"Coldiron used to be a trapper. In this snow he'd be hard to sneak up on and kill. He's also one of the best trackers in these mountains. I don't want to leave him alive to come after us. I want to sleep at night. Now here is my plan. We'll do this straight out. Just ride right up to him. Talk friendly like, kind of gather around him. You two Draguses being youngish-looking, he'll suspect least, so you get round back of him. Me and Tilston will keep his attention. The first second you have a chance, pull your six-guns and shoot him in the back. Blast his spine apart up high between his shoulder blades. A man shot there sure won't give you any trouble ever after.''

Tilston spoke in a mocking tone. "Have you Dragus boys ever pulled a gun on a real mean old lobo that could shoot the hell out of you in a tenth of a second?''

"You just watch us. We'll show you a thing or two,'' boasted Oscar. "After we do this job, I might just see how good you are.''

He turned and playfully slapped the brim of Vern's hat down. "We'll kill this Coldiron, right, brother?''

Vern grinned. "It ain't like we haven't shot several men before.''

Schiller spoke. "There'll be no fighting among you or I'll take a hand myself. Now there's an old man that works for Coldiron. Yerrington is his name. He used to be a gunfighter in his younger years. A fast one I've heard. But he's in his seventies now. He'll be slow and half blind I suspect. Watch him, but Coldiron is the one to kill first. Everyone savvy how this is to go?''

All three of the men nodded their understanding.

"Then let's find a trail down there below and go do it,''

said Schiller, and kicked his horse along the top of the rimrock.

Luke heard Cliff fire his rifle twice and reappear, coming back along the face of the snow wall. The old man called out, "Found two mares that were past help, so I shot them."

"Too bad," said Luke, and shook his head. "Maybe we can save the rest. I should have this path dug out to the shallow snow soon."

An hour later he straightened his back and glanced at the narrow trench he had made in the snow. "That should be wide enough for one to go through at a time. We'll have to scare the hell out of those weaker ones to get them on their feet. I'll get my rifle and let's give it a try."

All the horses watched as the men circled behind them. Luke signaled to Cliff. Both men pointed their weapons at the sky. Firing rapidly and shouting loudly, they rushed at the starving horses.

All the animals lunged to their feet. Slipping and sliding on the packed snow, they scrambled away from the frightening noise. The stallion lurched into the mouth of the cut chopped in the ice wall. The mares followed, staggering and careening off the sides.

In a minute all had passed beyond the drift and were wobbling off toward a patch of grass seed heads standing brown above the snow.

"I'm glad we came to the valley early," said Cliff, as he watched the famished beasts stop and begin to graze.

Luke raised his sight above the feeding horses. A knot of horsemen had come out of a grove of pine trees near the center of the valley and were riding straight for Cliff and him.

"Riders coming," said Luke.

"Now where did they come from?" asked Cliff. "What do they want?"

"Too early in the year and too much snow for most honest men to be out," said Luke. "Could be trouble. Get your rifle reloaded." He began to finger cartridges from his belt and punch them into the loading slot of his weapon.

"Where do you want to make our stand?" said Cliff.

"Right here on top of the drift where the snow has settled down firm enough for us to move, but not their horses.

They'll have to stop out there in the more shallow snow and come up to us on foot. You watch any of them that tries to flank us. I'll take the ones that stay in front.''

"Okay," said Cliff. He took station on Luke's right side. He unbuttoned his coat to make his six-gun ready as a second weapon.

The four riders rode at a trot. Snow splashed up from the horses' feet and trailed behind them in a little white storm. The lead rider, a tall man, waved his arm and shouted a hello.

Neither Luke nor Cliff responded to the greeting. Cliff said, "I don't like strangers who are too friendly."

The horsemen drew rein and climbed down from their saddles.

The man that had spoken grinned broadly. "You be Coldiron?" he called.

Luke nodded curtly in the affirmative.

"Then you're the man I'm looking for," said the man, and walked forward on the horse path with the others following.

They stopped when the side of the trench was waist high and climbed out to stand in the snow.

"I heard the shooting and thought you might be in trouble," said Schiller. "But I see you're not."

"Just getting some horses loose that got trapped by the snow," responded Luke. "What can I do for you?"

"Well, my name's Schiller. That's Ben Tilston and those two young pups are named Oscar and Vern Dragus. Me and the boys plan to buy some horses and drive them to St. Joe. Fatten them up there and have them ready in a month or so to sell to the wagon trains 'fore they leave to cross the prairie. I've heard it said you have mighty fine stock. You interested in selling a hundred head or so?"

"Could sell maybe a hundred. Pay would have to be in gold. I don't want any paper money."

"Yeah, I know paper ain't much good because of the war. We got gold there on that packhorse." He chucked a thumb over his shoulder.

"What kind of a trap did those dumb horses make for themselves?" asked Oscar. He waded the snow past Luke.

"I'd like to see, too," said Vern and trailed behind his brother's tracks.

They climbed up out of the snow and onto the ice shelf created by the weight of the horses' heads. Side by side, they looked down into the ice-floored arena.

Cliff cautiously watched the Dragus brothers as they stood on Luke's left, slightly behind him and twenty feet or so distant. Cliff felt his pulse quicken. The old gunfighter wariness in him began to heat. His thumb caught the hammer of his rifle and a finger the trigger.

He was worried, for his hands had grown stiff and clumsy during the last few years. Was he still quick enough to protect Luke's back? Once, such a question would not have entered his mind. Men such as these would have died easily.

"How much do you want for your ponies?" questioned Schiller. His voice was raised to a higher pitch to draw attention to himself.

The old gunfighter came instantly to keen alert. His shrewd eyes caught the tensing of the Dragus brothers. Two elbows suddenly showed from beside their bodies as they bent their arms to draw sixguns.

"Kill them," Cliff yelled at Luke and jerked up his rifle and fired.

The lead slug shattered Oscar's left arm and crashed into his chest. He toppled sideways against his brother.

With a curse, Vern thrust the falling body aside and completed his draw. Over the barrel of his weapon, he saw Yerrington hurriedly levering a second round into the firing chamber of his rifle. He shot the old bastard that had killed his brother.

Cliff doubled over at the punch of the bullet. He felt the hot wound that the lead had torn through him. His strength whisked away.

He caught himself from falling, bracing with all his might to stay upright. He had no hope of killing the second Dragus. All he hoped to do was stay on his feet as if only slightly hurt. Appear to be a threat. Above all, make the man waste valuable time to shoot him again. Luke must have that fraction of a second if he was to survive. Maybe even that amount of time was not enough.

Cliff felt his brain spinning. He was fearful he could not hold his feet.

The second bullet struck him. He fell, smiling a ghastly grin of success at Vern Dragus.

Luke sensed Cliff's movement even before the call of warning registered on his mind. His hands moved without conscious thought. His rifle bucked as he shot from the waist.

Schiller was hammered backward as the speeding lead projectile broke his heavy sternum bone.

Tilston's gun was nearly out of its holster when Luke spun the short arc and lined the sights up on him. The man's eyes opened large with fright in that instant of time before Luke killed him.

Luke heard the crash of a pistol, and a searing pain slashed his chest. He dropped to a knee as he whirled in the direction of the new attack.

One man still stood. He was hastily cocking his six-gun. Luke pointed his gun and pressed the trigger.

The man tumbled backward and fell heavily. Only his booted feet showed above the snow.

Hastily, Luke stepped to Cliff and lifted his head and shoulders. "How bad is it, pard?" he asked as he began to open his friend's coat and shirt.

"Bad enough to do me forever," answered Cliff in a calm voice. "They all dead?"

"Dead or dying." Luke examined the two wounds. Either one was grievous enough to kill.

"You hurt?" asked Cliff.

"Only a burn across my chest. Not serious."

"Good. I'm glad for that. Luke, I was slow. That pair should have been easy for me to take."

Luke ranged his view over the lined face. "You're a tough old rattlesnake. You did good."

"Luke, can you hear me? There's a noise growing."

"Yes, I hear you."

"You know the premonition that drew me back to the valley was not to free the trapped horses. I had to come here to meet death."

"I know, Cliff. I know."

"Bury me there by the ranch house near the garden. From there I can see down in the valley and watch the horses grazing."

"I will. I'll face you so you can see almost the whole ranch."

"Then all is as it should be, my friend." Cliff turned his head and gazed off at a band of horses watching from a ridge top. "They are indeed the best in all the New Mexico Territory."

"They truly are," agreed Luke and looked in the same direction.

They were silent together. When Luke returned his sight to Cliff, the man's view was fixed and unmoving. Gently, Luke laid him down on the snow.

Luke climbed to his feet. For the first time in many years he was the only living man in the valley. There was wetness in his eyes. He went to retrieve Cliff's and his horses.

Vern Dragus propped himself up in the snow. Sluggishly, he came erect, wavering back and forth. There was a terrible ache in his shoulder and his shirt and coat were wet with blood.

He spotted Luke watching him and he shouted out, "I give up. I'm shot and bleeding bad."

Luke cocked his rifle and waded through the snow toward the injured man. Dragus saw the ferocious anger, the desire to kill in the rancher.

"I've give up. I don't have a gun," Dragus called out in a frightened voice.

"What does that mean to me?" asked Luke savagely.

"You got to take me to Denver City for a proper trial. Or better, Santa Fe, that's nearer."

Luke laughed, a low guttural sound like the growl of a mountain lion. "Me take you to some town to stand trial? In this valley I'm the jury and the judge. You killed my friend and tried to kill me. You and I both know that. You're guilty as hell of murder."

Vern's voice rose in panic. "I'm unarmed. You can't just shoot me down."

"Sure I can," said Luke. "I am also the executioner." He raised his rifle until Dragus was looking directly down the black hole of the barrel. At death.

CHAPTER 2

The Arkansas River, Colorado Territory, March 31, 1864.

The rain turned to sleet as the two trappers whipped their straining horses up the steep grade leading to the narrow opening between the high shoulder of the mountain and the gorge of the Arkansas River. A cold wind blasted down from the north. It beat at the rock and pine covered ridges and slammed at the men with stiff blows, threatening to strike them from the slick trail.

Each man towed two packhorses, tied nose to tail. Large mounds of fur pelts—mink, otter, marten and wolf—were piled high on the laboring beasts. The ungainly, lurching loads yanked at the horses, trying to topple them from their feet.

Walt led, his bony old body hunkered down inside a wolfskin coat, the fur inside and the exposed side greased with bear fat to make it waterproof. He held his head tilted forward so that the sagging brim of his hat partially protected his face from the stinging grains of ice crystals.

He glanced right. The Arkansas River was three hundred feet directly below him, a boiling white cataract plunging through a vertical walled chasm. That impassable cleft in the earth had forced them to use the Arapaho Indians' ancient route that stretched from deep in the mountains down to the plains.

The old trapper's vision was restricted by the sleet to no more than a long rifle shot. Yet he knew with unerring certainty the location of the Wet Mountains lying four miles south and the Copper Mountains twice that distance north. Soon he and Virgil would be down out of the stormy mountains and riding swiftly east with their winter catch of fur.

The great number of skins would be worth many hundreds of dollars. That was a good thing, for Walt knew this was his last trip to this far, cold land. He was sixty-two years old and his days remaining on the earth had grown very few in number. All he wanted was to spend them quietly in a warm sun.

"Whoa! Whoa! You goddamn bastards," Virgil cursed shrilly.

Walt spun in the saddle to look behind. The last packhorse was reared up, its front feet flailing the air. The abrupt rocky edge of the gorge was only inches from his sliding hind feet.

Virgil began to strike his mount savagely with his rawhide quirt. The hurt beast lunged forward, dragging the nearest pack animal after it. The falling brute, tied to the tail of the horse ahead, was jerked down to its feet. It scrambled away from the precipice after its mates.

"Damnation, that was close," cursed Virgil.

The trappers fought upward. In the higher elevations the sleet became snow, falling heavily. The wind grew stronger and more erratic, darting first one way and then another around the serrated crests of the mountain. The hooves of the mustangs were muffled to stillness by the thick snow blanket. The hoarse saw of the animals drawing breath was masked by the tumult of the storm.

Walt forced his mount up onto the topmost height of the pass. He pulled a sudden, hard rein and came to a halt. All the horses behind stopped.

An Indian sat naked on the top of a tall boulder on the side of the trail. He faced east, away from the white men and into the curtains of snow that hid the foothills of the mountains and the distant great plains. He was as motionless as the stone beneath him.

Snow was piled like a white crown upon the top of his black-haired head. Heaps of the white crystals rested on each bronze shoulder.

"What are you stoppin' for?" shouted Virgil from the rear.

"Let's get on down the mountain to where it's warm." He crowded his cayuse ahead in Walt's direction.

The Indian twitched as if coming awake from a trance. Then he came erect with one fluid movement, spinning as he did so to face to the rear.

His sight jumped across the space to locate instantly the things that should not have been there. The black eyes flashed over the two trappers and the four heavily laden packhorses.

Walt saw the supple, ropelike muscles rippling under the dark skin. And he sensed the young warrior's thoughts as plainly as if they had been spoken.

They were dangerous thoughts for Walt and Virgil. The Indian had to be killed before he could do harm. The old trapper reached to throw off the cover that protected the rifle lying across the saddle in front of him.

Virgil sucked in a sharp breath of air and his hand snaked out for his weapon.

Almost too swiftly to see, the Indian bent to grab up a bundle of deer-hide clothing and a bow and quiver of arrows that lay near him. He stepped sideways from the rock and vanished downward.

"Shoot him," shouted Virgil. He sprang from the saddle with his rifle and rushed up beside the rock where the Indian had been.

"Nothing here," he called to Walt, who still sat his horse. "Plumb disappeared."

Walt leaned to catch the reins of Virgil's mount and rode forward. "Get in the saddle. We got to move fast." His voice was quick and tight.

"What's the matter, old man? He's just one Injun and with only a bow. He won't dare tackle us."

"You're a fool, Virgil. Ain't you listened to anything I've been telling you about Injuns these past two years. That there was an Arapaho buck. He's on a time of testing his strength and bravery. Probably been sitting there naked all day, maybe two days, in the snow and wind and didn't feel anything.

"He's searching for some deed to do to prove he's brave. Now he's seen our horses and furs. He'll try to kill us and take all that's ours. I know it. I saw it in him. We got to ride fast. Still, he'll catch us."

" 'Peared to me he ran like a coward. Anyhow, if he does

catch us, we'll shoot the hell out of him. You worry about nothing.''

Walt remembered the Indian's eyes. There was no fear in them. A man who had no fear of dying was the most dangerous kind of foe. Walt cast a vexed look at Virgil. The man would never grow to be old, for he was too slow to learn. It was good their partnership would end in a few days.

"That Arapaho wasn't afraid. He knew we had the advantage on him at the time. Get asaddle.''

"Hell, he didn't even have a horse. We can run off and leave him behind.''

"Even without a horse, he can run us down if he sets his mind to it." Walt struck his mount with the quirt and hurried along the narrow trail between the mountains and the river gorge and onward down the wooded eastern slope.

The old trapper and the young one halted in evening dusk and pitched a small hide lean-to among some pines. As they had descended, the snow had turned to rain. Now heavy drops fell upon the somber trees and dripped coldly from the edges of the sagging shelter.

A chilly, damp blackness crept in to obscure the boles of the trees. The wind whistled dismally through the long needles.

Walt climbed stiffly to his feet. "All right, saddle back up," he said in a hushed voice. "If the Indian saw us stop, he'll think we're spending the night here. Instead, we'll move on for a couple of miles and make camp in the dark where he can't see us.''

"You're crazy, Walt. The Arapaho won't bother us. And I'm just starting to dry out.''

"Virgil, I saw it in his face. I felt him decide to kill us. He's out there close. Can't you feel him?''

"All I can feel is wet clothes. I'm tired and I ain't going to move.''

"Then stay here. I'm going. Help me lift my fur packs up on my animals.'' Walt stepped close to the exhausted, slumped bodies of his horses to wait for Virgil.

"All right. Have it your way,'' grumbled Virgil. "I'll come with you.''

Later, in the deep darkness of full night, the trappers stopped under a giant ponderosa pine. Walt secured his animals tightly to the trunk of the tree with short lead ropes. He squatted beneath the heads of the horses and propped himself against the rough bark.

"Ain't you going to sleep?" whispered Virgil.

"Nope, not one eye wink. That Arapaho can come in on us at any time. With the horses helping us to listen, we maybe can be ready for him."

"Damnation, Walt. I've never seen you so scared before."

"Not scared, just plenty cautious. You would be too if you were a little smarter," retorted Walt. "Tie your animals same as mine and watch them for any sign they hear anything. If nothing happens tonight, we'll move out 'fore daylight and ride fast all day. Tomorrow night we'll sleep."

The trappers came down from the mountains in the late blackness of the night. On the low, rolling hills, they kicked their horses into a ground-devouring gallop. The dull rumble of the hard hooves awoke the sun.

The sound also guided Ghost Walker, the Arapaho. He followed behind, running at a speed that would keep him within hearing range of his enemies. When the sun first shoved its orange orb above the horizon, he slowed and dropped back so he would not be seen.

The rain had stopped during the night. The clouds had parted and the heat leaked away to the sky. Frost settled, cladding the old brown grass in a sheathing of white.

Now in the early morning Ghost Walker saw the hills glistening like new silver and sparkling with the sun's fire reflecting from millions of frozen crystals. The cool air was sweet and pleasant in his lungs. His breath plumed out from his nostrils like steam from a boiling kettle. It was a grand day for a battle.

He wished the white men would be strong and fight boldly so there would be much honor when he slew them. They were cautious. Ghost Walker had discovered that, for when he had stolen into their camp during the night, he had found them gone. He nodded his head in respect at their strategy. He judged the old one had planned that move to a hidden spot under the cover of darkness.

Ghost Walker continued to run into the day. Under the warming sun the frost melted and whisked away into the air.

The trees thinned, then vanished altogether, and knee-high grass stretched to the farthest reaches of his vision. The land grew nearly flat, with only slight undulations of its surface near the shallow watercourses.

The horsemen made no stop for food. However, when the sun reached its zenith, they slowed their mounts to a trot.

Ghost Walker carefully noted the course of the trappers. They had angled away from the river, an easy place to set an ambush with its trees and brush. That had been wise. Yet they had traveled a beeline route due east. That was foolish, for this was Ghost Walker's land and now he knew their destination. He veered off to the right at a moderate angle and increased his pace.

When the sun was barely a hand width above the horizon, Ghost Walker had drawn parallel to the trappers and a half a mile south of them. He had also run through the soles of his moccasins and his feet ached with stone bruises. Each step left a smear of blood.

Still, he lengthened his stride and hiked his speed to a gut-hurting race. Within the remaining daylight he must gain enough distance ahead to allow him time to select the place of the battle soon to come.

Walt and Virgil sat their ponies and surveyed the shallow swale, hardly two hundred feet across and covered with the tattered stalks of last year's growth of buffalo grass. A small spring, holding about three barrels of water, lay at the very bottom.

The old trapper raised his view to sweep it in all directions over the prairie. The sun had already hidden behind the Rocky Mountains. Overhead, the sky was fading to dark blue. On the eastern rim of the world, the heaven was deep gray and merging with the earth. Nothing moved within Walt's vision, clear to the horizon.

The day had been long. Walt's old muscles ached with fatigue and his head felt light and woolly. He wanted to bed down. Still, some warning worried the corners of his mind. He scanned the swale again, letting his eyes run along the broad trails worn through the grass by the buffalo, and the more narrow ones of the deer and antelope.

"Let's go down to water," urged Virgil. "We've outrun

the Injun. Now let's tend to our animals. Tonight I'm going to sleep like a dead man.''

The old trapper grunted as he hesitated.

Virgil watched Walt for half a minute. Then he shook his head in disgust at the double caution of the man. It was very strange, not at all like him. There was absolutely nothing to fear from the Arapaho.

"Well, I'm going," he said and guided his three horses down the slight incline.

Walt followed.

Ghost Walker raised up from the shallow trench on the slope east of the spring. The prairie grass he had used to camouflage himself fell away as he knelt on one knee and lifted his powerful war bow. The white men and the horses, intent upon reaching the water, did not see the Arapaho and took no alarm.

Silently, Ghost Walker watched the trappers, their backs to him, lie down and begin to drink. A more daring horse shoved up close and began to slake its thirst with the men. The others tossed their heads impatiently and waited.

The old man finished first and stood up. Ghost Walker pulled his bow to full draw and sighted at the center of the wolfskin coat. The arrow, its point armed with iron honed to a keen edge, leaped over the grassy distance, pierced the man from back to front and continued onward to stab deeply into the earth beyond.

Walt tumbled forward to fall with a splash, face down in the water. Virgil sprang up. As he came fully erect, a great searing pain stabbed through his chest. His lungs seemed to explode. Fire burned and raged within him. He dimly saw Walt's body rushing up at him as he fell upon it.

Ghost Walker still knelt, a third arrow nocked and bow bent, ready. The flight and strike of the projectiles upon the men's bodies had been clearly observed. His aim had been true. He released the tension of the bow and went to the dead trappers.

He lifted the corpses from the water of the spring and dragged them a short distance away. He dumped them unceremoniously on the ground and took the young trapper's moccasins and both men's skinning knives and pistols. The two

long-barreled rifles were retrieved from where they had been
laid on the ground while the two men had drunk.

Quietly, Ghost Walker waited for the horses to drink. They
were allowed to fill completely, for he would travel only a
short distance before halting for the night.

The last pony finished and lifted its dripping muzzle. Ghost
Walker climbed astride the old trapper's cayuse and rode up
out of the swale. He towed behind him the second riding
mount and the packhorses carrying his new fortune. Not once
did he look back at the corpses lying on the killing ground.

CHAPTER 3

By the evening of the third day after slaying the white men, Ghost Walker had crossed the Arkansas River and was a hundred miles south among the breaks of one of its tributaries, the Cucharas River.

His heart beat pleasantly, for he was almost home after two long, solitary winters. He lifted his head and breathed deeply, and for just a moment he thought he smelled the aroma of cooking buffalo meat on the slow gentle wind.

He guided the horses up to a grassy ridgeline from where the teepees of his people could be seen if the clan had used the ancient winter camping place. The instant he crested the rocky peak a boy lookout sitting a gray pony farther along the hilltop shouted a piercing warning down at the village of lodges strung along the bank of the river.

Ghost Walker imitated the familiar call, full-mouthed and strong, and then he began to laugh. "Little Turtle, is that the loudest you can yell? A sick old woman could do better than that."

"Ghost Walker, is that you?" exclaimed the young sentry, and kicked his pony in the ribs to send it scurrying up beside the new arrival.

"It is you! I must tell the others." Little Turtle sped down the incline of the hill toward the half hundred smoke-stained hide teepees.

Alarmed at the warning cry and fearing an imminent assault, the women dashed about crying out shrilly for their children to come to them. The braves with their weapons, mostly bows and arrows and a smattering of old muskets, came running to the near side of the village in preparation to move out and boldly meet the enemy.

"Ghost Walker has returned. He is not dead. He is not dead!" whooped Little Turtle, and slid his mount to a stop among the throng. He pointed up the slope at the man and horses.

As a victorious Arapaho warrior should, Ghost Walker rode in leisurely, his face composed and expressionless. His eyes drifted over the more than one hundred and fifty faces of the village, the tall men, the women watching him, and the children dancing excitedly around. He had not known how lonely he really was until that moment.

Where was the beautiful Bird Flying? She was the one who must see him arrive triumphant, with his riches of horses, furs and the white men's guns. He had dreamed of her many nights. Now it was time to go to her father, Broken Arm, and pay the marriage price for the lovely maiden.

Ghost Walker saw his uncle, Old Pony Man, who had raised him after his parents had died those long years ago. The old man smiled and nodded his approval.

Ghost Walker swung his searching sight. Bird Flying's parents were located, standing in the pressing throng, but she was not with them.

Then he saw her standing by Black Hand, the village war chief, and his wife. Ghost Walker raised a hand in greeting to the heavily muscled man and let his vision move to linger on Bird Flying.

The second their eyes touched, she wrenched her view away and looked up at Black Hand. The big man scowled and placed his arm possessively about her shoulders.

Ghost Walker saw the man's long fingers move to fondle Bird Flying's cheek. A cold wind blew through his stunned mind. She belonged to someone else. All his dreams of a proud return vanished. His heart felt crippled.

Someone slapped his thigh a stinging blow. Welcome for the intrusion into his sudden misery, Ghost Walker glared sternly down at the male child who had rushed in and struck this formidable warrior, counting coup to show his equally small comrades standing in a little pack of brown, wiry bodies what a brave fellow he was.

Ghost Walker remembered when once many years ago he had done the same thing and counted childish coup on Black Hand when that man had returned from a battle against the Cheyenne—the big warrior on a big horse, so high up Ghost Walker had had to stretch on tiptoe to make the blow.

They were men now and Black Hand had Bird Flying. She was the second wife and would always have to do the bidding of the first. Bird Flying deserved better than being a half slave to the woman. She deserved a husband of her own.

Ghost Walker threw a leg over the neck of his horse and slid to the ground. He walked through the crowd to stand by his uncle.

The people unloaded his furs and examined them, commenting upon the quality. Every single skin would be placed at his uncle's lodge. Warriors pulled the rifles from the scabbards and raised the long barrels to sight above the heads of the villagers.

Hunters, friends of Ghost Walker, left and returned before dark with the butchered carcass of a buffalo. The thousand pounds of meat were seasoned and cooked and a delicious feast prepared. The clan ate the succulent flesh of the buffalo and talked late into the night.

Ghost Walker slept late. Finally, he roused and lifted the flap of the lodge to go outside. People called greetings to him. The child that had counted coup on him squatted by the side of the teepee. His dark, liquid eyes full of hero worship followed Ghost Walker as he went down to the river to bathe.

Ghost Walker surged up out of the water and slung his long-haired head to shake the cold liquid away. As he dressed, he spoke to the boy that had trailed him. "Where is Black Hand this morning?"

"Black Hand and Bird have gone up there to the hills," responded the boy. "I heard him say he would kill a jumping one, a deer, and she took her digging stick."

Ghost Walker considered the information. Black Hand would have to go to the woods near the top of the hill to find a deer. Bird Flying would stop lower down at the marshes near one of the lakes made by the beaver. Several kinds of roots grew there.

"Didn't Bird used to be your girl?" questioned the lad, his brash eyes sparkling mischievously.

"Go home now," Ghost Walker ordered brusquely. "I have things to do."

Ghost Walker ran effortlessly, following the trail of Black Hand with ease. He was on foot because a man alone could hide in the smallest tuft of grass, while a horse could be seen as clearly as a mountain.

He came down from the grassland on the hill and into the cottonwood and red willow lining the creek. Ahead, he saw Bird Flying beside the large beaver pond. The water lay smooth, reflecting her kneeling figure and beyond that the mound of the beaver lodge. She worked steadily, oblivious to her surroundings.

At the beaver lodge the surface of the small lake undulated as one of the chisel-toothed animals left its snug hideaway within the mound of tree limbs and entered the water. The rippling wake crossed the pond, and the beaver rested its front feet on the bank and raised up to test the air with its keen nose.

The beaver caught the dangerous scent of the human on the shore. Like the crack of a rifle, the animal smacked the surface of the water with its strong flat tail and plunged back into the depths.

Not aware of the animal's close presence, Bird Flying leaped erect with a cry at the sudden noise. Quickly, she looked about. Then realizing what had made the sound, she laughed sheepishly and knelt again to her task.

Ghost Walker smiled at her pleasant voice. He circled the pond until he found the tracks of Black Hand's mount heading away. For a moment he stared along the trail, then headed toward the girl.

Bird Flying sensed the presence of some living thing very near. With her pulse racing, she sprang erect and whirled to the rear.

Ghost Walker stood watching her. His face was somber and his eyes sad. Yet there was a hardness, an anger about him.

For several seconds, Ghost Walker held Bird Flying's black

almond eyes, luminous as moons. Oh, how beautiful she
was.

He spoke in a husky tone. "Oh, Bird Flying, why did you
not wait for me as you promised?"

"I did wait," she cried out in a voice full of sorrow. "For
one moon after another. A whole year and then more. My
father pleaded with me to forget you and marry. Several
times braves came with many horses to my father's lodge.
Each time I convinced him he should allow me to wait a little
longer.

"My father said you must surely be dead, for why else
would a man stay away so long from the woman he wanted as
a wife. Then in the Moon of the Falling Leaves, Black Hand
returned from a long journey to the far Ute country and told
us those mean people had killed you. He offered my father
twenty horses and a white man's sword.

"In the Moon of the Strong Cold, my father said I must
take Black Hand as a husband. I have lived in his household
these past three moons."

"Black Hand lied, for you can see I am very much alive.
He tricked your father."

"Yes, I know now he did. We cannot prove he did it
purposefully. Even if we could, nothing would change. I am
his wife until I die or he forbids me to enter his lodge."

"Or until he dies," cried Ghost Walker. "I will kill him.
We can then go away to another village."

"No other village would accept us if you killed one of our
men for his wife."

Ghost Walker knew she spoke the truth. Anything he did
would be futile. "Then we have only one choice." He held
out his arms. She came into them swiftly, willingly.

He pressed her pliant body against him. His hand slid
down her back and caressed the soft curve of her waist, the
swell of her hips. Slowly, they sank to the matted grass
covering the ground.

He heard her whispers as they took their dangerous, forbidden love. Their strong young bodies thrust quick and hard, as
violent as a knife fight.

Black Hand tied the gutted deer carcass upon the back of
his cayuse and turned back down the mountain. It had been a

short, effortless hunt and he was glad, for there was an
insistent prodding in his body to return swiftly to his new
wife.

He moved on the trail through the woods, silently as the
glide of the hawk that soared overhead. At the border of the
meadow he cast a scanning view for Bird Flying. He immediately saw and heard the movement in the grass near the
beaver pond. He stopped abruptly and stood stone still. It was
Bird Flying and Ghost Walker doing the man-woman pleasure act.

The war chief wrenched his skinning knife from its sheath.
A low growl rumbled between his teeth as he moved swiftly
toward the two young people. He would kill them both,
easily accomplished as their minds soared upon the clouds. It
would be very fitting.

Black Hand caught his angry attack and retreated hastily to
the woods. His revenge must be greater than a fast stab of a
knife. For a moment he remained watching, his face fierce
and hot. He pivoted and went partway back up the trail. Then
he returned noisily along the path to the beaver pond.

Bird Flying was docilely digging roots as a proper wife
should. She kept her face down as they fastened her small
sack of roots to the back of Black Hand's horse. Riding
double on her pony, they left for the village.

In the long shadows among the teepees the flames of the
evening cooking fires glowed red and yellow. Women stooped
or squatted as they tended the food. Other women and children came in from the woods with heavy loads of fuel upon
their backs.

Ghost Walker sat beside Old Pony Man and watched his
aunt prepare the last meal of the day. His sight often strayed
to the trail that came down from the mountain.

"The sun has a misty face and it is getting chilly. It will
rain before morning," prophesized Old Pony Man, and he
nodded at the half-obscured sun. He pulled a buffalo robe
close and draped it over his shoulders.

Ghost Walker glanced at the sun, swelling as it touched the
horizon. He did not respond to his uncle. The man was a
great foreteller of the weather that was to come.

"I see Black Hand coming," said Old Pony Man. "He has killed a very nice deer. So why does he look so angry."

Black Hand steered a course among the lodges and the several people sitting or standing about. He stopped before his own teepee and sprang down from in front of Bird Flying. Without a word he stalked away from her.

Bird Flying climbed from her seat and went to the deer. She cast a quick, nervous look at Black Hand as she began to loosen the leather tie holding the deer on the horse's back. The man was acting strangely. Not once had he spoken to her during the return trip.

After half a dozen steps Black Hand spun about and swept the assembly of people with a fierce eye. He shouted a wild cry.

Every man, woman and child leaped erect and pivoted to see what was the trouble. Scores of other villagers poured from the lodges.

Black Hand bellowed again and flung out a hand to point at Bird Flying. "All of you look at that woman. I paid Broken Arm many horses for her. He gave her freely as my wife. She has lived in my lodge many days now. Yet only a short time ago, up on the mountain, I saw her lying with another man.

"The man who was with her is a dung-eating dog," cried out the war chief furiously, the veins of his neck swollen to thick cords. "He cannot win a woman for himself. He must sneak behind brave men's backs and steal their women away. I will kill him soon."

Black Hand whirled to face Bird Flying's father. "Your daughter is a deceitful woman, a bitch dog. I demand my twenty horses and the white man's long sword I took in battle."

The war chief's voice rose to a fierce howl as he continued to shout at Broken Arm. "I am going to do you a favor. An ugly woman makes the most trustworthy of wives. So I will cut a little of her nose off and she will cause men no more trouble."

The enraged man snatched out his skinning knife and leaped upon Bird Flying. His fingers caught the tip of her nose and he slashed with the sharp steel blade.

She wrenched to the side, striving to break away. Her sudden movement caused Black Hand to miss his mark, to cut too deeply. The honed metal edge sliced to the bone and then glanced downward, severing her nose and upper lip. The section of her face came free in his hand.

The pale ivory of the bone of her skull and the pearl white of her teeth showed, just for a second. Then the blood flooded out, a red tide spouting and cascading over her face and into her mouth.

Bird Flying screamed, a shrill, terrible screech of pain. She tried to run. Her legs would not hold her and she fell, to roll and twitch in her suffering.

Ghost Walker had seen the hatred in Black Hand and knew he would soon have to fight him, but the exploding viciousness of the man upon Bird Flying caught him by surprise.

In shocked disbelief, Ghost Walker vaulted to Bird Flying's side and knelt to hold her by the shoulders. He moaned in anguish at the sight of the hideous injury.

Bird Flying's fingers fluttered up to feel her wound, to unbelievingly explore the exposed, bloody skull. She tried to speak. Ghost Walker leaned close to listen.

A pleading whisper, searing in its agony, came from the crimson mouth. "Kill me," her tormented voice begged.

Ghost Walker looked into the stricken eyes. Eyes that had gazed with love upon him only so short a time ago. "I cannot do it! Oh, Bird Flying! I cannot kill you."

"You must. End it now," she beseeched him.

With a tormented shudder, he slid his knife from its scabbard. He placed the wicked point exactly over her heart.

"Please, do it quickly, my love." Bloody bubbles burst in the cavity of her mouth.

Ghost Walker positioned both his hands on the butt of the knife. With all his strength, he plunged the blade downward, cutting through muscle and bone to spear the frenzied, throbbing heart.

Bird Flying shivered and exhaled with a rush of air. Her breath did not come again. Ghost Walker's weapon had removed the gulf that separated the living from the dead.

Ghost Walker threw back his head and shrieked his sorrow. The squaws cringed and drew back at the dimensions of his misery. They began to wail the death chant.

Ghost Walker climbed erect. Hate for Black Hand filled his

mind until he thought it would explode. The man would know his revenge.

The war chief fastened a wary sight upon the younger man and held his knife ready. He waited for the attack he knew would come.

Ghost Walker rushed recklessly upon his foe. The war chief, wise in the way of battle, sidestepped and slashed out. The strike was short by the thickness of a shadow.

Heedless of his own danger, the young warrior whirled and sprang toward Black Hand. They grappled, each catching the wrist of his opponent, holding the other's knife away.

Ghost Walker's momentum was only slowed. He pressed his advance, his right leg stepping behind Black Hand, tripping him. They fell together.

Savage in his madness, Ghost Walker smashed his forehead into Black Hand's left eye. Then instantly into the right eye.

Black Hand arched backward, blinking rapidly. The dark eyes glared at Ghost Walker unimpaired. The war chief yanked his empty hand free and slammed the younger man a brain-jarring blow to the side of the head. The chief rolled to the side and jumped to his feet.

Ghost Walker tasted the gritty dirt in his mouth as he shook his addled brain. Black Hand was stronger than he. Soon that would lead to Ghost Walker's death. Unless he could think of something that would even the fight.

Ghost Walker opened his mouth and took a quick bite of the sandy soil. Instantly, he was on his feet and leaping aside to avoid the charge and the swift slice of the war chief's knife.

They closed, grasping at each other, their faces only inches apart. With a sudden spout of air, Ghost Walker blew the mouthful of dirt directly into Black Hand's eyes.

The blinded man tore free and jumped back. Digging at his pain-filled eyes with a hand, he sliced viciously back and forth with his blade. Ghost Walker poised his knife and swiftly moved to come in from the chief's side.

Black Hand struck right, exposing his left side. Ghost Walker drove in and plunged his sharp steel weapon to the hilt in the hollow at the base of the chief's neck. The man

quivered at the impact of the deadly blow. His arms ceased
their frantic motion. The legs folded and he collapsed.

Breathing raggedly, Ghost Walker surveyed the crowd.
Eyes began to turn hostile as they looked from the body of
Black Hand to Ghost Walker. Many of the braves began to
grumble. Some took up their battle lances with the heavy
wooden shafts. He had committed the unpardonable crime,
killing one of his own people. Worse, he had done so after
lying with the man's wife.

"Ghost Walker must pay for the murder of Black Hand,"
yelled one of the men. "Beat him! Kill him!" other voices
shouted. The squaws hastily retreated, pulling the children
with them. Among the lodges, they stopped, turned back and
waited. The men began to close a ring about Ghost Walker.

It would be a fatal mistake to let the menacing circle be
completed, Ghost Walker knew. He saw unarmed men grab
up lengths of wood from near the fires and heft them in their
hands as clubs. They would not cut or shoot him, however; in
tribal justice they would beat him to a battered corpse. He
could not fight his own people in turn. He sheathed his knife
to have his hands free.

A short, powerful man jumped forward and swung the hard
wooden shaft of his lance at Ghost Walker. Nimbly, the
young warrior dodged and the weapon swished past. Before
the man could recover his balance, Ghost Walker charged
him, ramming him and slamming him backward.

Ghost Walker drove through the temporary opening, el-
bowing aside another of the threatening braves. He burst into
an all-out run, dashing past the horse carrying the deer, turned
abruptly right and sprang between two lodges. Then immediately, he swerved left and raced down the narrow path separating rows of pyramid teepees. The sudden switches and turns
slowed his pursuers and gave him a few feet of head start.

He dashed from the encampment. Behind him the angry
voices clamored, high and shrill like a pack of hunting dogs.
Ghost Walker topped the first hill and sped down the far side.

The men would mount their fast mustangs and ride him
down. His only chance to escape lay in the string of timber
along the river. He bent his course to intersect that possible
haven before the riders overtook him on the open, grassy
hills.

*　　*　　*

The moon was pallid and misted and a cold, moaning wind walked the dark world. Ghost Walker was far down the river to the north of his village. His body was slick with sweat. Somewhere out there behind, his enemies searched in vain for his sign.

Ghost Walker rested. His escape had been a very close thing. A race to avoid death from men he knew well, had grown up with and called friends. How they must hate him.

Once just before dark as he crossed a high ridge, he had looked back at the place where he had grown up with Bird Flying and lived a pleasant, boyish life with Old Pony Man. A column of black, oily smoke had been rising. The people were burning his riches of furs. His horses would be slain and the white men's guns destroyed. Nothing of the Arapaho that murdered his own kind must remain. To the clan, he no longer existed, because they would either find and kill him, or failing that, never speak his name again.

Ghost Walker already felt the loneliness growing. He was now and forever an outcast from every village of the Arapaho. The message would spread swiftly. A murderer must never be trusted, never be invited to share a teepee or tossed a scrap of food. He was worse than any scavenging dog.

Taking a bearing on the stars, Ghost Walker plodded north. Far away on the border zone between the Arapaho and their ancient, enduring enemy, the Cheyenne, there was a no-man's-land. Both tribes avoided the vast stretch of plains and mountains, a mutual, unspoken agreement never to erect a teepee there, so that an endless war did not destroy both peoples.

There Ghost Walker would live and die. With every man his foe, he did not think he would survive long enough to grow old.

CHAPTER 4

The Wilderness, Virginia. May 5 and 6, 1864.

A mighty host of 200,000 soldiers in gray and blue fought a ferocious battle. Union 5,597 killed, 21,463 wounded, 10,677 missing. Confederate 2,000 killed, 6,000 wounded, 3,400 missing.

A blood-red sun exploded up above the hazy horizon and mounted a long, high trajectory through the sky. The bright rays stabbed into the thick forest of pine, cedar and scrub oak. In the strong earthen redoubts on the high ground, the sergeants of artillery bent to sight the black iron barrels of their long weapons.

In obeisance to the giant cannonball climbing the sky, a thousand cannons opened fire along the lines of the opposing armies. *Krumph! Krumph!* The earth shook. The battle began its second day.

Musketry stuttered as scouting parties probed the enemies' defenses. Quickly, the racket grew to a crashing din of rifle fire as companies and whole regiments threw themselves into the conflict.

In ten minutes a pall of gunpowder smoke rose in dense clouds over the shallow valleys and clung like ground fog on the hills. In an hour the sun had been dimmed to a wan moon. The pale sphere hung overhead, uncaring of the men dying below the shroud of yellow-gray smoke mist.

Jubal Clason, scout for the 94th Ohio Company, and temporarily attached to Headquarters Command, ran with long strides among the trees of the forested and broken land. Sweat soaked his blue uniform and washed muddy tracks down through the grime, thick on the sharp planes of his face. He had lost his hat in the battle of yesterday and his shaggy hair trailed out behind in a black mane.

The air lay still and dead on the hillsides and in the swales. The cannon and rifle smoke was bitter in his nostrils and his lungs burned with its acid. Above the roar of the guns, he could hear nothing, not even the pound of his own falling footsteps.

The leather strap of a dispatch pouch went over his shoulder and the bag hung beneath his left arm. A .44-caliber Colt pistol was strapped to the center of his chest where it would not interfere with his movement and slow his pace. The black wooden butt of the weapon slanted to the right, ready to his hand.

Jubal passed soldiers in singles and groups. A lost corporal, leading three other men, shouted out, "Runner, wait! Where is the command post?"

A very young private looked up from where he was cradling the head of a man equally youthful, and yelled shrilly, "My buddy is bleeding to death. Where is the ambulance wagon? Where is the hospital and doctors?"

The scout ignored all of their entreaties and passed swiftly by. Minutes spent to help these men would delay the message he carried and could cause the death of a thousand soldiers.

In a grassy clearing he saw a white tent. The flaps were open on both ends. Inside on a wooden table a soldier lay. He was strapped down and two burly men also held him tightly. A surgeon was hurriedly pulling a short steel saw across the bone of the soldier's shattered right leg just above the knee. He finished. One of the male nurses threw the severed member onto a pile of legs and arms, waist-high to the scout.

An ambulance wagon pulled by a team of trotting horses came out of the woods with a moaning load of wounded. It passed the dead wagon hauling a bed full of corpses toward a long, open trench. Jubal swung his eyes away.

The course turned upward for two hundred yards. At the top he dodged around a large oak, full of hanging wild grapevines, and came out onto a flat bench mostly free of trees.

Jubal maintained his speed toward the regimental command post, set up under a lage canvas tarpaulin stretched between four tall pine trees. Several officers were grouped around a table littered with maps. A squad of command guards with rifles at the alert stood nearby with a drove of saddled horses. A covered wagon used to haul the command's paraphernalia of signaling devices, maps and ciphers was drawn up close to the canvas.

The sergeant of the guard recognized the scout and motioned him to come straight in. Colonel Cuplin strode out half a score steps to meet the scout and impatiently took the dispatch bag.

The colonel paced among his staff as he read the single sheet of paper. He finished and raised his view to his subordinates. He shouted out above the noise of the guns firing along the ridge and down in the valley. "Gentlemen, Lee has not been dislodged and is holding firm. Headquarters estimates his Army of Northern Virginia at eighty thousand strong. We have him outnumbered by about twenty thousand. I bet General Grant is smiling. He will never ease the pressure on Lee.

"We are to swing our western flank to the south and take Big Gurney Ridge. Then position our artillery to fire to the southeast. Lieutenant Caldwell, to the maps. Let's see what we have to contend with to capture that place."

The lieutenant quickly began to study one of the several maps on the wooden fold-up table. "Here, sir," he said, and thrust his finger down upon the cloth map.

The colonel leaned over to inspect the symbols and writing. "It's Captain Mugridge and his boys from the Ohio 94th and Huddelston with the Indiana 5th that will have to do it. They are in the best position to advance swiftly and hit the Rebs before they are aware we are moving."

The *whump* of a 24-pound, smooth-bore cannon directly opposite on the Confederate lines jarred the air. All the Union officers twisted to look in that direction. The projectile whizzed overhead and burst in the trees higher on the hill.

Colonel Cuplin's face hardened. There was an almost imperceptible shrug of his shoulders. With a wave of his hand he caught his staff's attention and motioned them to the table. They began to discuss tactics among themselves.

The scout had not turned to face the cannon. Looking

would not change its point of aim. He slumped more heavily against the bole of the tree. As he watched the officers, his face was bleak and his eyes glittered with some emotion not fully concealed.

What were the generals, Grant and Lee, thinking as they ordered attack, feint, counterattack against each other on a battleground so choked with brush and trees that from no point could more than a thousand soldiers be seen. Blind men striking at each other. Did the generals know the numbers of the dead? The millions of years of human future destroyed?

Jubal was sick to death of the uselessness of the fighting. The reason for the war had seemed so clear when he had enlisted in Cincinnati a year ago. He had laughed and joked with the other new soldiers as they marched. They spoke of freeing the black man and preserving the Union. That was all bullshit now. Had been even then.

He had left the fur-rich valley of the Arkansas River in the Colorado Territory early in the spring. In St. Joe he sold his winter catch of furs. Normally, he would have spent a few days lavishly enjoying women and whiskey in that city and then gone on to hunt the great herds of buffalo on the wide plains. Instead, he had headed east to join the Union Army and have a magnificent adventure.

The war was not magnificent, it was an ugly thing. The two armies were locked into a battle that was a self-perpetuating and all-destroying ritual. A horrible deadly game played between Grant and Lee. Maybe they got some thrill out of the contest between them. If they did, while killing tens of thousands of men, well then, goddamn them both to hell!

Jubal had killed men before, several of them. He had fought Indians for land to trap upon. He and other trappers had gone into Mexico to recover stolen horses. They had shot seventeen Mexicans and he had felt good about it. Also, a man could slay another for a woman or for gold. These reasons were easily understood.

This war between Grant and Lee was for nothing. All these dead were a terrible waste. What was he doing here? He must be as insane as the others.

"Clason! Damn it, man, can't you hear me?" The colonel called sharply.

Jubal jerked his senses to attention. "I hear you," he growled.

Colonel Cuplin clenched his fist at the tone of the scout's voice. His sight clashed with Jubal's. The scout showed his teeth in a mirthless grin.

The colonel made a silent promise. When this battle was over, that soldier was going to receive some hard lessons in how to show proper respect to an officer. But then a second look into the scout's marble blue eyes sent a wave of doubt through the officer. It could be dangerous to reprimand the violent scout.

Cuplin kept his voice strong as he shouted out. "Then get your ass over here. I want you to take this message to Captains Mugridge and Huddelston. Can you find them?"

"The Ohio 94th is my company. I always keep track of their whereabouts. I understand the Indiana 5th is just east of them."

"That is correct. Here is your pouch. Make it a fast trip. Stay there and report back to me when Big Gurney has been taken. Or if that has not been accomplished by dark, report to me anyway with full details of the situation. I have written those same orders to the captains. Now on your way."

The Confederate sniper crawled to the center of the valley and into a clump of tangled and broken trees, a copse of pine and scrub oak mutilated by the ferocious cannonading of the early morning. Through the long brass tube of the telescopic sight of his rifle, he surveyed the low wooded hill rising before him. Near the top of the ridge was a six-gun battery of 12-pound Napoleon cannons. The guns, strategically placed among the trees, were being entrenched with earthen embankments thrown up by blue-clad men with shovels.

The sniper minutely examined his enemy in the magnified field of the sight of the .45-caliber Whitworth. He estimated the range at five hundred yards. At that distance and from a solid platform he could place a bullet into the chest of a man with no great difficulty.

From under his belt, the sharpshooter pulled a pad of folded burlap, laid it atop a horizontal log, and rested the heavy rifle upon it. He found a half-comfortable position and rested, patiently waiting for the Yankee artillery officer to grow careless and expose himself to the fine, long-barreled killing rifle.

The thunder of battle lay on Jubal's left. The gunsmoke now completely hid the sun. The men tending the cannon, and the soldiers crouched with their rifles behind the log and dirt barricades, paid no attention to the man running past through the smoke clouds except to check the color of his uniform.

Jubal broke from the woods and out into a clearing of an acre or so overlooking a shallow valley. He jumped over a dead man, puffed and bloated in death. The fetid stench of death took Jubal's breath. He slowed and looked around.

A hundred more bodies lay strewn in awkward, grotesque positions. Caught in the open meadow by cannon firing canisters of shot, the men had been scythed down like weeds by the murderous flying metal. Flies in a black fog swarmed and droned about the corpses, feeding on the rotting blood and flesh.

"Water! For God's sake, water!" cried a garbled voice from a mound of bodies.

Jubal spotted the source of the pain-filled plea, a soldier with half his chin gone. One of his hands had been blown away. The stump was tied with a crude bandana tourniquet. He was a man that should have already died from his wounds.

The Confederate sniper, hidden in the trees on the floor of the valley, saw the movement in the clearing at the base of the hill. He locked the telescopic sight of his rifle on the enemy soldier. When the man turned, the Rebel sharpshooter saw the dispatch pouch.

He grunted with satisfaction. A courier had more priority to be killed than an officer, unless it was a general.

The sniper centered the cross hairs in the magnified field of his weapon upon his foe, held his breath and fired.

Jubal recognized the man as one of the Ohio 94th. He was going to die and water would not stop that. Yet Jubal could not turn away from a man he had marched with for a thousand miles. He turned to look for a canteen. He saw one at his feet and leaned to pick it up.

Jubal felt the hot slash of the bullet across his back and heard the distant, sharp crack of the heavily charged sniper's rifle. He leaped away. In two strides he was in a flat-out, dead-streaking run.

Dodging and weaving, he crossed the rest of the clearing and plunged into the protective cover of the woods. He left the level bottom land and began to climb the hill beyond. The wound on his back began to burn as if molten lead had been poured on it.

Finally, in a shielding clump of brush, he halted and bent an arm behind to feel his injury. His shirt was torn and bloody and he found a bullet groove, long as his finger, in the flesh of his back. Only the movement of stooping to retrieve the canteen had saved him from being dead now.

He took a deep breath and let it out with a sigh. He was a stupid fool. There was absolutely nothing to be gained here in this eastern land. He faced the hill and moved upward. A plan was forming in his mind.

The Ohio 94th should be close. He knew he was correct when a battery of Napoleon 12-pounders sounded off above him. For a moment he listened to them, each gun working rapidly, two shots per minute, shaking the hillside.

On the opposite rim of the valley, Confederate mortars opened up, returning the fire. Ground-thumping explosions worked their way up the slope toward the Napoleons, searching for the correct range.

Jubal came into sight of the nearest Union cannon. The artillery men, seven ghost men in the billowing smoke, hurried to load powder and ball, and poke a lighted wick to the touchhole. The cannon roared and lurched backward.

The Rebel gunners continued to lob shells, canisters with explosive charges, lighted fuses and seventy-eight musket balls packed inside in sulphur. Jubal heard their whizzing flight as they arched down through the air.

A pair of shells burst with two brilliant orange flashes upon the nearest Napoleon. Musket balls and hot burning sulphur hurled in every direction. The cannon and the limber that held it were hit. Wood, iron, and human flesh exploded simultaneously. One of the lead musket balls hit a tree with a wicked *thunk* near Jubal.

He dashed forward. The artillery corporal hung over the

axle of the broken limber, his entrails dragging on the ground. The powder man who had been nearest the shells had been struck with a score of balls and was a bloody, limp hulk plastered against the dirt embankment. All five of the remaining tenders lay crumpled and mangled.

Jubal stopped and stood very still, surveying the carnage. None of these men would need any help. He began to curse Grant and Lincoln, Lee and Davis.

"Clason, over here," someone called.

The scout pivoted. Captain Mugridge and First Sergeant Owens rode out of the woods on the side of the hill.

The captain roved his view over the destroyed cannon and its crew. He grunted once and spoke to the scout. "Give me the dispatches."

Jubal ripped the strap from around his neck and threw the pouch to the officer. Immediately, he faced west toward the far distant Colorado Territory. In his mind's eye he saw the tall mountains, the broad grassy plains, a land of clean breezes free of the rancid stench of the rotting flesh of men and horses. He began to walk.

"Clason, you haven't been dismissed," barked the captain in a surly voice. "Where are you going?"

"To Colorado," Jubal shouted over his shoulder.

"Stop!" Mugridge commanded.

Jubal did not slow.

"Halt, you goddamn coward. Halt or I will put a bullet through your spine." Mugridge pulled his revolver and cocked it.

Jubal whirled around. He stretched a crooked smile across his mouth. "I'm no coward. I'm afraid of no man. Nor any two men." He ranged his sight over the sergeant sitting with his hand on his holstered pistol.

"I've had enough of this war," said Jubal. "During the last year I've killed better than thirty men who had nothing I wanted. I'm going west. Mugridge, you and Owens come with me. We have fought enough."

"No one is deserting my command," shouted the captain. "I will kill you if you try."

Jubal moved to the left three steps to better see the sergeant and at the same time to put the head of the captain's horse between him and the open end of the gun barrel.

"Sergeant, would you shoot me, too, if I was to leave?" asked Jubal.

Owens glowered down from his horse at the scout. "You enlisted for three years and you'll serve three years. Unless you are killed."

Jubal lengthened his smile to show all his teeth and began to laugh. He clasped his stomach as if in merriment and bent forward, chortling loudly. His right hand, hidden from the two men, slipped up to grasp the butt of his six-gun.

He suddenly straightened, sliding the pistol clear of its holster. With a quick swing he brought the weapon up to bear on the startled face of the captain. Jubal fired.

The bullet broke the bridge of Mugridge's nose, plowed through the gray brain matter, and blasted out the rear of the head, tearing away a section of skull big as half a hand.

Instantly, Jubal rotated to bring the pistol to point at Owens. The man hurled himself to the right from the saddle and a hand clawed for his revolver. The scout's shot went in under Owen's ribs, punctured the soft lungs, destroyed the heart and broke the clavicle as it tore out the top of the shoulder.

The two horses whirled away from the falling bodies to be halted by the steep side of the embankment and stood nervously tossing their heads.

Jubal cried out wildly at the dead men. "Damn you both to hell! Since you like the dead so much, then go live with them to eternity."

The scout controlled his savage anger. Carefully and swiftly, he reloaded the fired chambers of his six-gun.

Hastily, he bent to search the dead men, taking money and pistols. He stripped off the officer's four-button field jacket with the golden insignia of a captain on the shoulder and tugged it on. An officer would be less likely to be questioned as to why he was leaving the battlefield.

Jubal bent again over the captain, removing the riding boots and exchanging them for his flat-heeled shoes. He donned Mugridge's black hat and went to the horses.

A new Spencer eight-shot repeating rifle was in a scabbard on the sergeant's horse. Jubal grinned in genuine pleasure at that discovery. He tied up the reins of the mount and put a lead rope around its neck.

He climbed astride the captain's horse, and looking neither left nor right, went up over the ridgetop, passing several soldiers, and down the far side. The woods were soon left behind, and he picked up a dirt road leading west over farmland. A company of fresh foot troops, sweating heavily, came past at a double quick pace. Jubal returned the salute of the young lieutenant commanding the soldiers.

Jubal Clason spoke to the dead captain's horse. The strong beast picked up a swinging lope. The sergeant's mount readily matched the pace.

When the road veered north, Jubal held a course due west. Just eighteen hundred miles and he would be home. He would make only one stop, to take something very valuable from a man in Missouri.

CHAPTER 5

Missouri, August 8, 1864.

In the deep woods Jubal tied his mount and the packhorse carrying his steel traps and winter supply of provisions. On moccasined feet, he slipped soundlessly onward through the dark forest of giant beech and oak.

He stopped in the deep gloom beneath the trees at the edge of a clearing and scanned ahead. A three-quarter moon cast a pale silver light down into the opening in the woods. In the center a log cabin was a blurred, squat outline. A square field of some cultivated crop that Jubal judged to be corn lay close to the right end of the house.

With a low grunt of satisfaction at finding the homestead peaceful and slumbering, Jubal dropped his rifle into the crook of an arm and leaned against the bole of a tree to wait. A plump-bodied bug, frightened by the man's sudden approach to its nighttime hiding place, whirred up from the bark of the tree and darted into the moonlit clearing.

A bat, swooping in on its jerky, speedy flight, pursued the insect and caught it in an instant. With one crunch of strong teeth, the tiny predator devoured the tasty morsel.

Jubal tracked the bat until it vanished from sight in the darkness, then swung his eyes to continue surveying the farm. Around him the forest began to whisper as the fingers of a breeze rustled a million summer leaves. Jubal cocked his head to listen warily behind him as he continued to watch to the front. Enemies moved when the wind made noises.

The wind worked its way deep into the woods and its noise died. Silence flooded back.

Jubal left the deep shadows of the forest, crossed a short stretch of grassy meadow and crept into the cornfield. Dew fell damp and cool upon his skin when he brushed the long, bladelike leaves of the corn stalks. At the end of the row he seated himself behind a concealing clump of horseweeds and stared at the cabin.

Come morning he was going to kill the man that lived there. That decision had been made a year earlier as he had been heading east to join the Union Army. He had stopped and knocked upon the door of the farmhouse, intending to borrow tools to reset a shoe that had come loose on his horse. Even now, a year later, he felt his blood speed as he relived that moment when the woman opened the door and he saw her for the first time. The remembrance of her full lips smiling at him and her eyes widening in a gentle, inquisitive manner was clear and strong. He stopped the images, held them in his mind, savoring the beauty of her. A man could kill to possess a woman like her.

The eastern sky showed the faintest graying, heralding the sun's imminent arrival from below the far horizon. The moon gilding on the house grew dull and tarnished as the dawn brightened. The single glass windowpane on the front of the house started to shine dimly. Two hundred yards beyond the farmhouse, through a swath of girdled and dead trees, the water of the Missouri River glinted weakly.

A horse nickered in a lean-to shed behind the house. A second one answered.

Jubal continued to wait. He silently broke an ear of corn from the stalk nearest him and pulled back the green husk. The kernels, swollen in full ripeness, popped between his teeth. The sweet milk filled his mouth with delicious flavor.

He chewed slowly, relishing every small, rich tidbit. A second toothsome ear followed the first.

Jubal heard the brief, cautious noise as the rough, serrated edge of a corn leaf scraped against something. The sound stopped. Jubal sensed the presence of someone else in the field. More than one, at least two, off on his left.

They stirred again, coming nearer. Jubal noiselessly swung

the barrel of his rifle to point where they would appear in the open. The odor of unwashed bodies reached him.

Halting in the border of the field, the men began to whisper. From not ten feet away, Jubal listened to the hiss of their voices.

"Charlie, we might miss him from here with just our pistols," a man said. "Damn. I wish I had a rifle."

"Well, we don't," said a man Jubal assumed would be Charlie. "We'll have to get close. There's no window on the end of the house. We'll sneak over there and jump him when he first comes outside for his morning piss."

"May not have to shoot at all. Save our bullets and just stick a knife in him," said the first man.

"Yeah. Then grab his money, saddle his horse and get on out of here," said the first man.

Jubal began to smile mirthlessly. These thieving rascals were going to do the killing for him. Then he would shoot the hell out of both of them. If he handled this correctly, the woman would think him a hero and savior. Jubal almost laughed out loud. Who ever said there wasn't such a thing as luck.

Slinking low, the two men furtively hastened from the cornfield to the wall of the house. One went to a corner and peered around at the front door. The second looked past the opposite corner at the rear entrance. They turned back and grinned with grim humor at each other.

Jubal waited and watched the two. There were hundreds of men such as these on the western border. With large numbers of husbands and brothers away in the eastern armies, the ruffians and bully-boys had become bolder and were now robbers and killers. They were rarely caught.

The iron lid of a cook stove clanked within the cabin. The occupants were awake. The men in ambush sprang to each corner to see which door the man would use to come outside.

A large, young, barefoot man dressed in cotton pants and shirt came through the front entrance. He glanced casually both ways and walked away from the house.

Jubal rose to a shooting position with one knee on the ground. The farmer had no weapon. Fool, thought Jubal, you deserve to be killed.

The attack came swiftly. The men leaped from hiding and with knives drawn, rushed upon the unsuspecting victim.

Hearing the charging feet pounding the ground, the farmer pivoted. Immediately recognizing the danger, he shouted a piercing cry of warning at the house and raced for the open door.

His assailants reached it first and whirled to face him. Without the slightest hesitation the young farmer hurled himself at the nearest armed man.

Jubal watched in astonishment the man's fearless charge upon the would-be killers. It was the only thing the fellow could do unless he were to desert his family. Still, it was a bold and grand thing to see.

Charlie slashed crosswise at the farmer's throat with his knife. With a quick twist, the man dodged aside. The steel blade missed its intended mark and sliced into his upper arm.

The farmer whirled back and swung at Charlie. The strike was short and he missed. He broke off his attack and jumped from in between the men as the second man came in from behind.

Dismayed at the farmer's courageous resistance, Charlie yanked out his pistol. "Mack, get back," he shouted. "I'll shoot this crazy son of a bitch."

"He sure is one wild bear all right," said Mack. He saw movement behind Charlie as someone appeared in the open doorway. "Watch out behind you," he shouted.

A young woman with a long-barreled rifle clutched in her hands rushed outside. Charlie spun around. So near was he to the cabin that the woman was upon him before she could slow.

Charlie ducked to the side just as the gun discharged. The gray plume of powder smoke engulfed him from the waist up.

Charlie appeared out of the smoke, shaking his head, trying to stop the ringing in his ears from the explosion of the weapon.

Mack stepped forward and struck the woman a blow with the barrel of his pistol. She fell heavily.

"Goddamn," cursed Jubal when he saw the woman go down. She was not supposed to be hurt. But there was something else. She had run clumsily and her stomach was swollen and distended. She was with child and her time was near.

She moaned and sat up. Jubal saw the blood on her face. Awkwardly, she started to rise.

Enraged at the injury to the woman, Jubal lifted his rifle and began to shoot. The shots slammed into Charlie and Mack, slamming them with invisible blows, buckling their legs. Before they had fallen, Jubal was out of the cornfield and running across the clearing.

He knelt beside the woman and tenderly put his arm about her shoulders to steady her.

"It's okay. They are both dead," he said. "You are safe."

She looked up into Jubal's face. He felt a surge of pleasure, for she recognized him and the fear left her eyes.

"Oh, it's you," she said in a hesitant voice. Then quickly she swept her gaze to her husband.

Blood gushed from his arm and his face was ashen. He took a tight grip on the wound with his hand, but still the blood poured from the injury.

"Please help me stop the bleeding," said the woman, and struggled to her feet.

"Yes, ma'am, I can do that," said Jubal. "Give me a strip off the hem of your dress." He bent and ripped off a length of cloth. A tourniquet was swiftly tied around the man's arm and drawn tight.

"Will he be all right?" asked the woman.

"Sure, he'll be fine. We'll need to sew up this cut, for it's too deep to heal right by itself. Find me a needle and some thread."

Jubal finished the task of closing the raw edges of the wound. He paid no heed to the man's pain, only telling him roughly to hold still when he flinched at the punch of the needle.

The woman brought a tin of salve and Jubal liberally applied a coating of the amber substance to the stitched flesh.

"You are skilled. You must have done such a thing before," said the woman in a pleased tone.

"Yes, ma'am. Several times." He handed the salve back. When she reached to receive it, Jubal clasped her small, brown hand in his and held it.

Her fingers trembled against his palm and she stared into his eyes. Jubal wondered what she was thinking.

Jubal knew the man was observing his hold upon the woman, but he did not care. He only knew the woman made his chest ache with longing. Yet his plan to take her with him was ruined. She could never travel the long distance to the Arkansas River and on up into the mountains.

Jubal released the woman's hand and regarded the farmer. There was now no use to kill her husband. Let him live to care for her.

Jubal turned away without a word. There was nothing here that he could have. He retrieved his rifle from the ground. With long strides he crossed the yard and the meadow beyond and entered the woods.

The Arkansas River, Colorado Territory, November 17, 1864.

A hard blue sky lay to the east behind Jubal. Ahead, over the distant Rocky Mountains, high, thin clouds of ice crystals heralded the near approach of a storm. Already a faint nimbus was gathering about the early afternoon sun.

A flat plain covered with short prairie grass surrounded him on all sides. It stretched away for mile upon mile until finally broken on the west by the uplifted flanks of the Rocky Mountains. The Arkansas River was an hour's ride to the south, far enough distant so he could most likely avoid the Arapaho Indians coming down from the mountains to set up their winter camp in that sheltered valley.

Jubal had journeyed steadily since leaving Missouri, traversing the six hundred miles of plain that slanted upward at a gentle angle to intersect the base of the mountains. He had encountered half a dozen groups of white men. Little time was wasted talking with them. However, they had warned him the Arapaho and Cheyenne were on the prowl, raiding small wagon trains, stages and isolated ranches. The few platoons of soldiers not recalled to fight the great battle in the East could do little to halt the attacks.

The white men had also told of large discoveries of gold in the mountains near Denver. Trading and building were booming. The population was increasing substantially. Neither the war nor the Indians could stop the flow of men crossing the land to hunt and probe for the elusive yellow wealth.

Jubal had seen small groups of Indians at a distance. They had all sat their mustangs and watched him pass, except for one bunch of four that had followed for half a day before turning back and disappearing into the back trail. He encountered scores of buffalo herds and the great white wolves that fed off them. The buffalo drew back both left and right like the parting of a black surf to let him ride through. The wolves pulled away even farther and watched him intently.

A puff of north wind swirled past, riffling the grass and whispering the dry reeds together. There was a touch of chill in the air. Jubal pulled his coat from behind the saddle and shrugged into it.

He spoke to the captain's horse and the obedient brute lengthened his step. The packhorse kept pace. Already thirty miles had been made good this day. Yet the season was late and there was still a very long way to go to the mountain stream that was to be trapped during the winter. A cabin had to be built and meat laid in for the moons of the short days.

He crossed the sandy bottom of a dry creek bed and climbed the ridge beyond. The horses stopped of their own volition to rest. The clouds were heavier over the mountains. The topmost peaks, white from the snow of an early winter storm, blended into the clouds, and it was impossible to distinguish earth from sky.

Jubal's mount twisted its head and looked to the left. His ears thrust questioningly forward. Jubal turned his sight in the same direction.

A large band of Indians had popped out of some low, hidden swale and was racing toward him at a full run. From a quarter mile distant, they were twenty or so miniature painted men on miniature running mustangs. Aimed with deadly intent at him.

He saw their arms rise and fall as they swung rawhide whips to flog their wild mounts. The sound of the hard hooves reached Jubal as the horses struck a rocky area of land.

Jubal spun his steed, curled two quick dallies of the lead rope of the packhorse around the horn of the saddle, and tore off in the opposite direction. In three strides his mount was running full-gait.

The Indians were dangerously close. And far too many to hold off alone. His only chance of escape was to outrun them. Yet he guessed the ponies of his foes were fresh while his were half used up.

A mile fell away. He could plainly hear the savage cries of the braves above the pounding thuds of his horse's feet. His enemies were gaining.

The lead rope to the packhorse was taut with tension, holding back his mount. If he continued to tow the slower animal, he would surely be caught and killed.

Jubal slowed and fell back beside the second horse. He reached out and yanked loose the flap on the left pack. His searching fingers jerked out the buffalo sleeping robe and draped it over the saddle in front of him.

He threw off the turns of rope to free the pack animal and the weary beast slowed. Jubal boiled on ahead. All his supplies for the winter were gone. He glanced back and saw one of the Indians turn aside to catch the packhorse. The man shouted with glee.

Jubal touched the stock of his rifle. Someone would pay dearly for that.

He dashed over the top of a rise and saw a long rock outcrop blocking his path. His horse could not climb it. Hastily, he scanned to both sides. Abruptly, he veered left to wind a curving course up and through the obstacle.

Jubal saw the Indians dash straight ahead, passing over the obstacle along a route he had not seen. This was their land. They gained ten horse lengths.

He leaned far forward and screamed into his horse's ear. Stretching every tendon, the valiant beast lengthened his stride, his nostrils flaring and sucking at the air.

The race was hard-fought as Jubal and the Indians ran through the afternoon. Jubal accommodated every move of the gallant steed, bending low, positioning his body just so over the powerful chest and driving front legs to lessen the burden of carrying his weight.

Sweat lathered the withers and flanks of the splendid brute and formed a white, frothy ring around his mouth. Yet he forged onward, holding his lead.

A cold wind swept in, blowing hard from the north. It struck squarely into Jubal's face. The temperature was below freezing and dropping swiftly. Wind tears puddled in the corners of his eyes.

Thick clouds sped in, lowering, putting a lid on the land. Two miles ahead, misty streamers of snow started to fall from the dark, gray bottoms. The mountains disappeared, swallowed by the growing storm clouds.

Jubal ranged his sight over the sere, frigid emptiness of the prairie. There was no place to elude his pursuers and hide. Unless he could endure until the storm hit. He lifted his whip for the first time and lashed his blown and weakening horse.

The Indians had also seen the storm and recognized the chance for escape it could provide their quarry. At a sharp call from their chief, they began to flog their cayuses savagely.

Jubal heard them shouting urgently for their steeds to pick up the pace. They were so near he could see swirls of steam breaths from the men and their ponies.

The leading edge of the storm swirled over Jubal. Diamond ice, hurled against his face, stung like flame. He ducked his head to protect his eyes.

The snow grew more dense. The Indians became hazy silhouettes behind the white curtain. Jubal hurried away from them and into the protective bosom of the storm.

Electrical charges built up within the snow torrent. Sheet lightning flashed, a smoldering, unnatural glow trapped within the falling white cascade. Thunder rumbled, and for an instant Jubal thought it was a buffalo stampede about to erupt from the unseen world beyond the storm and overrun him.

He ran his horse through the turbulence and murk of the snowstorm. Now was the moment to shake the Indians from his trail. He swerved aside at a steep angle.

The millions of blowing crystal flakes blinded even the keen-sighted horse. He could only guess where to plant his hammering feet. He made a wrong guess and his right hoof plunged down between two rocks embedded in the frozen ground. The hard hoof, driven with a force of thousands of pounds, became wedged, locked within the crevice.

The momentum of the half ton of hurtling horse broke the ankle bone with a sickening snap. Man and animal crashed down, cartwheeling end over end.

CHAPTER 6

Jubal was bruised and jarred by the fall upon the hard ground. His head rang and he had difficulty catching his breath. He tested arms and legs. There were no broken bones, and he rolled to his knees and stood up.

He scurried to his horse and dragged the rifle free of its scabbard. A quick check showed the weapon was unbroken. Hastily, he dug a box of ammunition from a saddlebag and crammed it into a coat pocket. Scooping up his sleeping robe from the ground, he dashed away into the snow.

The two warriors came like phantoms from the billowing whiteness on his left. Jubal's rifle leaped like a live thing as he shot twice, knocking both Indians from the backs of their horses. Other wavering, indistinct figures appeared. One saw him and yelled shrilly. A bullet zipped past. A feathered shaft with a jasper point sliced the side of his face.

Jubal bolted through the snow, making sharp left and right turns to evade the Indians. Their calls faded away behind him.

He swerved straight into the teeth of the storm. With legs and arms pumping, he left that hazardous place.

Above him the sky was an ocean of streaking, tumbling white. The snow was swirled up from the ground in a blinding haze. He ran, feeling his way from the touch of his feet upon the ground. Now and then through short breaks in the storm, his nearly frozen eyes could dimly discern the snow-plastered prairie lying before him.

He raced on, his lungs pulling hard to catch the swift air

59

and his heart beating great pulses of blood. He held the frigid
north wind on the front of his face and hoped the Indians
would not search into that freezing gale. He slipped and fell,
jumped up and continued to run.

Miles later Jubal slowed to a steady trot. His breathing fell
off to a bearable level and his heart decreased to a durable
beat. The pace could be maintained for many miles.

His hat had been lost when the horse fell. Now he draped
the end of the buffalo robe over his icy head and shoulders
and, pulling the opposite corners around his back, tied them in
a crude knot in front.

The cold intensified. The wind grew to a hurricane, blowing directly from the birthplace of blizzards. The storm whipped
him, eating away the warmth of his body.

His muscles began to stiffen with fatigue. His head felt
light and woolly.

The gloom within the storm deepened to gray. The day was
ending. Just when Jubal had decided to stop and seek a place
to lie down, the wind eased and the snow slackened and he
could see several hundred feet around.

He stopped and stood with the snow flowing and rippling
around his ankles. Ahead, a bank of water vapor rose up from
the ground. It froze quickly to ice crystals and moved off
with the wind. He had never heard of hot springs in this part
of the plains. Yet there were many thousands of square miles
white men had never seen. Such a place of heat, if it existed,
would make an excellent spot to sleep.

As he drew nearer to the mist, a dark mass at its base
became visible. A moment later he identified the source of
the cloud. It was rising from a vast, closely packed herd of
night-bedding buffalo. The animals' breaths, condensing rapidly in the supercold air, was creating the ice fog.

There must be thousands of the big shaggy beasts, thought
Jubal as he roved his sight over the multitude of bodies. He
crouched low and edged forward. The wind was from the
animals to him, and he came to the very perimeter of the herd
and not one member detected him.

The wind picked up its vigor and the snow increased. The
dusk was almost night. What better location could be found
to sleep the darkness and the storm away than among the

shelter of the herd. If it could be done without stampeding the lot of them.

Two cows lay side by side and facing off ninety degrees from the wind. In the lee between their bodies, the snow had drifted, nearly burying their two calves of the past spring.

Jubal crawled in from the rear, squeezing tightly into the small space separating the calves. One raised its head and sniffed at the tanned, smoky hide robe. A strange-smelling buffalo, yet still the friendly, safe scent of one of his own kind. The calf again rested its head beside its dam and went back to sleep.

Jubal wrapped himself and his rifle in the thick fur of the sleeping robe. It encased his body snugly, soft as heavy velvet.

He heard the arctic wind moaning an endless dirge as it walked the dark world. Felt its cold fingers clawing at his protective covering, searching for an opening so it could come inside with him.

Jubal laughed. He felt good, deep down where his real being lived. His enemies had failed to kill him. The frigid storm was held at bay an inch away. For the strong such as he there was nothing to fear.

He went to sleep in the black wintry night.

The wind tumbled down from the forested slopes of the front range of the Rockies and across the arroyos, cutting through the foothills. It buffeted the three riders and switched the long tails of the band of horses they drove.

Luke Coldiron buttoned his coat tightly against the cold and scanned the crowns of the three-mile-tall mountains on the left. Massive cloud banks were building on the high, stone peaks and spilling eastward toward the plains.

Luke shouted out loudly and circled his arm above his head. The two horse wranglers heard and came spurring toward him. The herd of mustangs came to a halt.

"It's going to snow hard in a short while," said Luke. "When it does, we won't be able to see much, and in this broken up land we will lose several of these horses."

"I would guess so, too," agreed Andy. He reached up and cinched his hat down more firmly over his red hair as a stiff gust of wind flopped the wide brim. "It could be one mean blizzard with all this air."

Luke spoke. "Denver is six or seven miles ahead. Let's run the ponies the rest of the way. We have a chance to get there before the storm catches us."

The second wrangler shifted in the saddle and skimmed the land to the north. "Mighty rough country to cross at more than a walk. Could be some animals will have bad falls."

"Best we gamble some, John," said Luke. "I've got a contract to deliver eighty horses to Wilber Kerr. I plan to keep it. We can't stand to lose any more than the three that drowned at the river crossing. I'll take point. You fellows bring up the two flanks. Stay far enough back to act as drivers, too."

Luke touched his horse with spurs and circled to take station in the lead. With a shout and an overhand motion to the north, he left at a trot.

Behind him he heard the sharp yipping cries of the wranglers urging the herd of horses to start. Soon the rumble of hard hooves sounded above the noise of the wind.

On the flat terrain the herd sped at a full gallop toward Denver. The horses slid and jumped into the occasional arroyos blocking their course and scrambled up the steep sides, throwing gravel from beneath their feet.

Luke spotted Denver, a bleak clutter of buildings on the flat, treeless prairie. He guided the course toward the big log corrals on the east side of the town.

Two men left the cabin near the end of the enclosure and hastened to throw open the wide gate and then position themselves to help funnel the running herd inside.

Luke led the animals directly into the round structure, circled close to the walls and went back through the open gate just after the last mustang entered.

"Well done," shouted Kerr, a big, dark man, as he swung the gate shut. He shoved the locking pole into its slot and faced Coldiron. "How many do you have?"

"We started out with eighty and three extras. Lost those three crossing the Purgatoire River. Still have the eighty head you and I bargained for."

Kerr climbed up on the top of the corral wall. Luke and the wranglers joined him.

As the men looked across the corral at the horses, hard, icy splinters of snow began to fall, angling in on the strong wind. The horse buyer lifted his hand to protect his eyes and keep his vision clear. He said nothing for several minutes as the horses ceased milling and quieted. He minutely examined each one.

Finally, Kerr spoke. "Dozen or so are skinned up some."

"Just scratches. Nothing serious," said Luke.

"Are they saddle-broke?" asked Kerr.

"Saddle-broke is all," answered Coldiron. "They're not trained to stand for roping. I've heard there's been new gold finds since we agreed on the price. I'd think horses should be bringing a premium now. Men have to get over much country to do their prospecting."

"There's plenty of gold right now. I can probably sell all the horses before folks figure out there's not as much gold as they think. The price of a hundred and eighty-five dollars a head we agreed on still stands."

"I'll take gold and all coin if we can find that much."

"The full payment is ten thousand dollars. Why do you want so much coin?"

"Easier to count and handle. I plan to play some cards for a few days at the Elephant Corral. I will need part of the money for that."

Kerr wiped snow from his eyebrows. "Damn fine weather to be staying indoors." He jumped to the ground. "I might stop over to the Elephant and watch how the poker game goes with you. Let's go to the bank and I'll draw out the money to pay you."

In the lobby of the Kuntze Brothers Bank, Kerr paid Coldiron twenty pounds of gold coin and was written a bill of sale for eighty horses in exchange.

"Good to do business with you, Coldiron," said the horse trader. He touched his hat in salute and pushed the door open against the storm. A squall of snow spun inside as he left.

Luke counted out gold coins and handed a palm full to each of his wranglers. "You fellows are top riders. You can work at my ranch anytime."

"Thanks," said Andy, accepting his wage and shoving it into a pocket. "John and me are going to loaf this winter and then in the spring go prospecting. But if you ever need hired hands, well, look us up. Could be we may be flat broke and ready to throw a rope again.''

John nodded agreement to his partner's statement. The men ducked their heads and went out into the snow and the wind in the street.

Luke walked up Larimer Street and entered the newly built Charpiot Hotel. He had seen its foundation being laid in the spring when he had visited Denver to make the horse contract. He had promised himself to try it at the first opportunity. The structure was a large, three-story building with an elegant lobby and thick wool carpets on the floor. The odors of recently sawed wood and fresh paint were strong and pleasant.

He registered and stowed his heavy pouch of gold in the hotel vault. While he soaked leisurely, and half slumbered in a tub of hot water in the bathing room in the rear of the hotel, a Chinese laundryman washed his clothes and pressed them dry with hot irons. They were still warm from the iron as Luke slipped into them.

Luke reflected upon his rough and worn garments. He was moderately rich and could afford much better. He made a mental promise to purchase a new outfit before he left Denver.

His room on the second floor was frigid when he entered. The glass window panes were rimed with hoarfrost. He slid open the wooden slat in a section of the floor to allow the warm air to ascend up the hot-air plenum from the giant fireplace on the ground floor. He judged there would not be enough heat from that source, so he lit a pinewood fire in the small iron stove in the corner of the room.

For the first time in many days, Luke slept between clean sheets on a soft bed. In the late afternoon he arose, buckled on his six-gun and went down to the lobby. A delicious meal was obtained from a richly provisioned buffet in the dining room. Afterward he counted out an even two thousand dollars from his gold hoard and returned the remainder to the vault for safekeeping.

The snow was falling more heavily when he went out into the street. Wind whirled it along the ground, drifting it in the wind shadow at the corners of the buildings and piling it behind the barrels and boxes on the sidewalk. The few horses that had been left tied to the hitch rails were like ghost animals, covered with white from sheets of snow sticking to their hairy winter pelts.

Coldiron came upon scores of freight wagons drawn up in two parallel lines close to the side of the street. Men were working swiftly unloading wooden barrels from the canvas-covered conveyances. With grunts of effort the workmen shouldered the containers to carry into a large cavernous warehouse.

One man slipped and fell, dropping his burden. The barrel bounced and rolled away.

Luke caught it with his foot and held it against the slant of the grade.

"Thanks, mister," said the workman as he got up and brushed at the snow on the seat of his pants. "It's damn slick. I sure wouldn't want to bust that open and waste ten gallons of good whiskey."

Luke looked at the numerous heavily laden vehicles. "Are all of those wagons hauling the same goods?"

"Yep. Eighty wagons have come from St. Joe and brought sixteen hundred barrels of whiskey and twenty-seven hundred cases of Champagne wine. We had twenty guards and all the drivers to see the Indians didn't take it away from us. Going to be one wet and lively winter in good old Denver City."

"It would appear so," said Luke. He went out into the center of the street to avoid crossing the path of the working men and continued on his way.

Denver was growing into a fair-size city if the people needed that much liquor and wine, thought Coldiron. The population must be approaching five thousand residents. Many hundreds had arrived each year since the town had sprung up out of the desert with the discovery of gold in 1859. The Civil War in the East had slackened the migration across the plains; still, the people came in droves to search for the elusive gold, or in some way profit from the army of prospectors.

The clank of an operating printing press came through the wall of a building with a sign declaring it to be The Rocky Mountain News. Farther along the street, a message on the Holladay Overland Mail and Express Company read, No Stages Until Further Notice—Indian Trouble.

As Luke crossed the South Platte River on a pine-plank

bridge, a wagon piled high with lengths of fuel wood clattered past. The driver shouted a hello down to him and popped his bullwhip at the team.

Coldiron deliberately cut through Hop Alley, the town's Chinese section. He had always been intrigued by the quiet, withdrawn men and their small, pliant women. He sniffed the air. Mixed with the damp smell of the snow was the faintly sweet odor of opium smoke.

Luke entered Blake Street, a thoroughfare lined with saloons, gambling parlors and whorehouses. Several men and women passed him with hasty steps along the wooden sidewalk.

He came to the Criterion Hall Saloon, built in the first flush of gold madness. It was the toughest place in all Denver, the major hangout of the meanest ruffians and outlaws in the Territory. Coldiron went on past, for he did not want to stumble into a fight, rather only to enjoy a few hours of playing poker.

The Denver House, better known as the Elephant Corral, was filled with a press of people. The evening festivities had started early because of the storm. Most of the patrons were miners and prospectors, but freighters, shopkeepers, woodcutters and meat hunters crowded about. Saloon girls served all of them except those standing at the bar. The place reverberated with the rumble of the deep voices of men punctuated now and then with the shrill soprano of one of the women.

Luke spread his hands to the warmth of a tall, round cylinder stove. It was cherry-red with heat. Even the thin, tin stovepipe was red and seemed ready to melt for a yard or more up its height. He turned his back to it and looked about.

The Elephant Corral was one giant room some thirty feet wide and a hundred feet in length. It was built of long light-colored cottonwood poles with a slanting, skeleton roof, like the rib cage of a mammoth beast. All was covered with a skin of loose canvas. With the pull and push of the wind the rough fabric billowed in and out with a rasping sound against the logs. Three stoves similar to the one near Luke were spaced along the floor to heat the windy building.

In the barroom just off the street Coldiron stopped and drank a bourbon. Near him an orchestra composed of a fiddler, a cornetist, a fifer and a pianist were playing "Sweet Betsy from Pike." On a square wooden dance platform raised above the tamped earthen floor, two miners and the red-headed cowboy, Andy, danced with brightly dressed saloon girls. Andy halted, and holding his girl by the hand, threw back his head and with his face filled with rapture, yodeled for a full minute, using up a lung of air. He stopped, caught his wind and swung his companion back into the dance.

Beyond the barroom and dance area, the space in the room was taken up by playing tables—faro, blackjack, monte and poker. All were aligned in three long lines with aisles between them. Bob Teats, the owner of the Elephant Corral, leased the tables to professional gamblers by the week or month. For twenty-four hours a day money and cards changed hands across the boards.

One of the men at a faro table called a greeting to Luke. He returned it and wound a course to the far end of the room and the poker tables. Every seat was occupied.

Bob Teats, moving in his patrol between the barroom and gambling hall, raised his hand above the heads of the throng to signal a welcome.

"Damn, what bad luck," cursed a poker player. He slapped his cards down and got up. "I sure can't beat you," he said to a handsome, very blond man.

"Better luck next time," said the blond man.

Luke dropped into the vacated seat. From his money belt he began to extract gold coins. As he stacked them in neat piles on the green felt-topped table, Luke examined the other players.

The gambler was known to him only by name, Sandy Sanderson. He was a small, nervous man. The next two chairs were taken by miners, with callused palms from the handles of shovels and every fingernail splintered and broken from picking rocks out of the sluices and cradles used to wash out the gold. The blond man was on their right. A Union cavalry captain in uniform was on Luke's left. There must still be soldiers stationed at the army garrison near town, surmised Luke.

"Straight five-card draw," Sanderson informed Luke. "There's no wild cards, no limits to size of bets or number of raises."

"That could get to be a rough game," observed Coldiron.

The blond man looked at Luke's faded and work-battered

clothing. "It is for those who can't back their hands with hard money."

Coldiron chuckled. "I probably got the money to stay for the ante of a few hands," he said.

Sanderson grinned. He knew of Coldiron's ranch. The blond man saw the gambler's smile and more closely evaluated the black-haired, blue-eyed man of forty or so. Nothing extraordinary. Just a cowhand.

Coldiron lost slowly and steadily. He played a conservative game or his pile of gold would have been gone. He studied his opponents.

Sanderson played unpredictably, sometimes folding quickly, then unexpectedly with a flourish raised again and again. Coldiron thought the gambler ran a strong and successful bluff now and then.

The two miners were cautious men, clumsy with the cards. The blond man had supple white hands. It seemed to Luke the fellow deliberately made his actions more awkward than they would normally be. The cavalry officer was wound up tight, and intent on winning. He seldom did, and the quantity of money before him had dwindled to less than a hundred dollars.

A hand of cards ended with the blond man winning. He raked the mound of coins from the center of the table. Scooping up the cards, he tapped them on two edges to square up the deck, and placed it in front of the captain to shuffle and deal.

Coldiron rapped sharply on the tabletop with his knuckles. He reached out and hammered his clinched left fist down upon the card deck, making the table jump. His right hand dropped out of sight to rest on the butt of his six-gun.

"Give me a card count!" he demanded tersely of the captain. "I believe the deck is short."

CHAPTER 7

"Count the cards out. Count them slow so everyone can see," ordered Luke, raising his fist from the deck. He did not look at the captain. His eyes appeared unfocused, yet his attention was centered on the blond man. He watched for a shift of body, or a movement of muscle that would mark a man trying to shed himself of a card.

The officer glanced around the table at all the players. Everybody looked steadily back.

"Count the cards," directed Sanderson impatiently. "Any player has a right to call for that. All the cards had better be in that deck. I run a straight game and aim to keep doing so."

Sanderson had also thought there had been an odd motion of the blond man's hands. However, the man was quick to anger and was very fast with a six-gun, had proved it several times in the few short weeks he had been in Denver. Let Coldiron call for the count and do the shooting if it came to that.

The captain began to count, piling the pasteboards with their red backs in a mound on the green felt cloth. "Fifty-one," he said, laying the last one slowly and deliberately down all by itself.

Coldiron's tone was brittle as he spoke. "Somebody has a card stashed somewhere. For the sake of that person's health, I suggest he get up, leave his winnings and get out of here. It would be very wise if he never came back. Now whoever has the card, put it on the table."

Silence held. Not a man moved to respond to Coldiron's command.

At the adjoining tables, men had twisted around to watch. Some of them nervously climbed to their feet and began to draw away to a more distant and safe place.

One of the miners called out in a strained voice, "You can search me. I don't have a card."

"Me either," said the second miner. He unbuttoned his shirt sleeves, rolled them up and pulled out his shirttails.

"How about you?" Luke spoke directly to the blond man. "You got a hidden card?"

"I don't answer questions like that," snapped the man. "And nobody searches me." His hands slipped close to the edge of the table.

As if going to let the matter rest with the blond man, Coldiron faced the cavalry officer. "You're next, army man. You got a card hidden somewhere?"

Coldiron began to rise as he asked the question. Before he was fully up, his hand flashed into sight with his six-gun. The open bore of the weapon was pointed straight into the face of the blond man.

The handsome countenance became instantly ugly with anger at the trick that had been played to throw him off guard. The speed of the cowboy's draw astonished him.

"Now sit easy, fellow," said Coldiron. "Make no moves or you are a dead man."

"Sanderson, go round there and look through his clothes."

The gambler circled the table and ran his hands over the man's lower arms. "Nothing here so far."

"Keep looking," said Luke.

The man sat rigid as Sanderson felt along his belt. The gambler chuckled as he brought a card into view. "He has a little secret hideaway pocket sewed into the front of his shirt. Now ain't that slick. Been cheating, playing with six cards instead of five like the rest of us."

"Take his pistol and empty it," Coldiron directed Sanderson.

"You will pay for this, cowboy," growled the blond man.

"Not as much as you," replied Luke. He called over the heads of the standing men to Bob Teats, who was making his way forward to find out what was happening. "Damn poor place you run here, Teats. Can't a man have an honest game?''

Teats looked piously heavenward. "Pray, what has all this got to do with me. The professional is supposed to stop any cheating.''

"I see how it is," said Luke. He moved his sight to the cheat and spoke in a flinty voice: "Get up and walk straight out of here. Leave your winnings right there. Don't ever let our paths cross again.''

"There's over three thousand dollars there," muttered the man as he climbed slowly to his feet. "I'm not being robbed that easily.''

"Robbed!" exclaimed Coldiron. "You are nothing but a goddamn thief. I gave you your chance. But you argue when you would have been better off moving out of here. Empty your pockets and throw all your money out there on the floor so that anyone that wants to can pick it up. I suspect all of it is stolen, too.''

"You are crazy. I'm not going to do it.''

Luke swung his view over the crowd gathering about. "All of you fellows that have played with this man, why don't you just strip him of all of his stolen loot and throw him out the door so we can get on with our card playing.''

A pack of men swarmed upon the helpless cheat. A large burly man knocked him to the floor. Eager hands ransacked his pockets. The man who had struck the sharper went straight for the money belt and came up with it dangling in his hands.

"Just about what I lost," he laughed without counting its contents. He pivoted and swiftly left the Elephant.

Coldiron watched the hurried exit of the man. The others that had set upon the blond man quickly followed the first through the door.

Luke noted the men seemed anxious to be gone from the hapless victim. As if afraid.

"Throw this crooked gambler outside in the snow," Teats called to his bouncer, a square-built man with massive arms.

"You should have killed him," the saloon owner told Coldiron as the unconscious man was dragged away. "He's a mean one and will not let this end without getting even.''

Coldiron shrugged and turned to Sanderson. "I believe you saw the card being palmed and did nothing about it. Well,

I'm going to teach you a lesson. I'm going to bankrupt your damn game before this night is over and send you out to shovel manure for a living.''

Luke raked all the blond man's gold into a pile before him. "I'm going to use the sharper's money to do it," he told Sanderson.

In the cold gray dawn, the herd of buffalo gradually began to stir in their snow beds.

The resting beasts were just ahead of Ghost Walker as he snowshoed through the huge white drifts carved and hardened by the winds of the night blizzard. His body was bent far forward at the waist to be parallel to the ground. A buffalo hide hung over his back and dragged on the snow. A strong, thick-shafted bow was clutched in his left hand and an arrow was nocked ready to draw.

He came up to the buffalo slowly, stopping often and pawing with his left hand at the snow. No unusual actions must be made that would frighten the animals.

A small white buffalo wolf, a pup of the past spring, saw the undersized, awkwardly moving creature approaching the herd. Thinking it to be a crippled, young buffalo, the wolf dashed in from the rear to make its attack.

Ghost Walker heard the crunch of snow beneath the padded feet and pivoted to strike at the beast with the end of his bow. The wolf sprang aside and, catching the alien odor of the human, retreated in haste. His ungainly pup's legs became entangled in each other for an instant and he almost fell. Then he was running full, long strides.

The Indian crept close to the herd. Some of the buffalo were standing and gazing with interested but unfrightened sight at the strange figure with the loose hide.

Ghost Walker knew that sometimes a herd would allow a man in such a camouflage to walk right among them. At other times they would stampede at the mere sight of such an unfamiliar form. He came in very slowly.

An inquisitive quarter-grown calf rose up from where it was lying in the snow and came a few body lengths nearer. For Ghost Walker alone the four hundred pounds of flesh would be sufficient for many days. The young animal would be very tender.

He knelt and drew the bow to full curve with the fletching

of the prairie hawk feather brushing the side of his cheek. He
released his draw. The bowstring twanged. The sturdy flint-
tipped arrow smashed through the unhardened bones of the
immature beast's rib cage, entered the chest cavity and pierced
the throbbing heart. With a weak bleat for its mother the calf
sank into the snow.

Jubal Clason slept as cozily in his buffalo robe as does the
grizzly bear in its depth of fat and fur. When the calf arose
and removed its bulk from beside him, Jubal came awake. He
lay listening with his head still covered.

The wind voices that had argued during the night were now
silent. He could plainly hear the step of the calf in the brittle
snow.

The death cry of the young buffalo reached Jubal. He
sensed the hurt in the plaintive sound. He took hold of his
rifle, sat up and flung aside the buffalo robe, to send flying
the snow that had drifted upon him.

Jubal saw the Indian stooping over the body of the calf and
withdrawing an arrow. Even as he had that first glimpse of
the warrior, the man spun to stare at him.

Instantly, the bow lifted up and the bloody arrow that had
killed a moment before was nocked again, and the point
pulled to touch the shaft of the bow.

Clason wrenched his long gun free of the robe, rolled to
the left and leaped erect. With one swift motion he hoisted
the weapon, cocking it before it reached his shoulder, and
pulled the trigger.

There was no explosion of the gun firing, only the click of
the falling hammer striking the faulty carriage. That sound
was smothered by the noise of Jubal's feet on the snow.

Clason froze in the shooting position, looking down the
sights of the rifle at the Indian. The man must not find out the
gun had misfired. Bluff him until there was an opportunity to
lever in a fresh shell to finish the fight.

Ghost Walker, in his hurry to nock his arrow, had struck
the string of his bow with the glass sharp-edge of the flint tip.
The twisted sinew had been nicked and weakened. Then as he
bent the bow with powerful force, the tough cord parted,
leaving him unarmed.

He retained his stance and grip on the bow and the fletching of the arrow resting in its proper place against his face. He prayed to the Great Spirit that the white man would not see the amount of curve in the bow was only that which had been permanently imprinted into the wood from being bent hundreds of times.

Clason watched the Indian, waiting for the pointed shaft to come zipping at him. At this short range of twenty yards, there was no chance the man would miss.

The Indian did not shoot. The seconds drifted past. Jubal began to evaluate the warrior that did not kill when he had the opportunity. For two winters Jubal had lived with an Arapaho woman. For another season a Cheyenne girl. On this border between those two tribes, this warrior would be from one or the other of those people. Jubal judged him Arapaho.

The Indian was lightly dressed for such cold and snow. His buckskin clothing was crudely cut and sewn, as if made by some inexperienced hands. Perhaps by the man himself. His body was thin, lean as a whippet hound. He could probably run just as fast. The black eyes intently staring across the point of the arrow showed no fear, hard as obsidian.

The knowledge of the presence of the strangers had worked its way through the buffalo herd. All the animals found their feet, and hundreds of hairy nostrils and sharp eyes pointed at the rigid forms of the two men. Gradually, the buffalo lost interest in the unmoving objects and began to amble off.

The minutes slipped by slow and weary as Jubal held the defective rifle aimed at the Arapaho. The steel and wood in his hands, that had seemed light as air at first, increased in weight to a thousand pounds. Sweat began to trickle down the center of his back and bead in large drops on his forehead.

The sun came up from its hiding place beyond the flat, treeless horizon. From a cloudless blue sky the bright sphere centered behind the Arapaho. A target surrounded by a golden halo. If only Jubal could shoot.

His muscles started to quiver with the strain of propping up the gun. Still the Indian braced the bow with the arrow fully drawn back. As if it were a toy bow, like the children play with. Yet the wood at the grip was half as large as his wrist.

Clason realized he was beaten, for the gun now weighed a full ton, too heavy to support a second longer. He spread wide his arms to fully expose his chest. He shouted out in the Arapaho tongue, loud enough to be heard for a mile.

"Arapaho, let loose your arrow. This white man is not afraid to die." He began to laugh at the irony of the situation. A thousand rifle bullets had missed him and a hundred cannon balls. Now he was to be killed by a wooden splinter tipped with a piece of stone.

Clason shook his arms to emphasize his impatience. "You are stronger than I am, so finish the contest." He showed his teeth through his black beard in a smile. "Do your damndest," he called in a final command in English.

Ghost Walker watched the white man in amazement. He had expected at any moment for the gun to roar and strike him dead. Now the man held wide his arms and asked to be slain.

Then the Indian understood. The white man would only behave in this manner if his weapon was broken. Each man had cunningly deceived the other. Ghost Walker began to laugh. He turned his bow to the side to show the loose and broken strands of the bow string.

Jubal laughed even harder, pounding his thighs in glee. Tears came to his eyes. He flicked them away with a finger.

He held out his hand, palm toward the Arapaho, the sign of peace. The Indian was one damn brave man. Brave men did not always have to make war.

Ghost Walker gave the same sign in return.

"Great," said Jubal. "There's no reason for us to fight each other. The prairie is wide and more than large enough for both of us." He advanced, holding out an open hand toward Ghost Walker.

The Arapaho took the extended hand, clasping it firmly and returning the shaking motion of the white man. A peculiar custom.

"You are correct. The land is broad and the buffalo are many. We will not fight." He motioned to the calf and gave the sign language for eating.

"Good idea," agreed Jubal. "Let's find a creek where there will be some wood and cook a large batch of that meat."

Ghost Walker knelt by the side of the dead buffalo. With a few deft strokes of his knife, he sliced along the ridge of the calf's back and peeled the hide away. Both narrow strips of the tenderloin and ten pounds of haunch were removed and laid into a carrying pouch.

The Indian straightened and started cross-country. As he walked, he dug out a spare sinew and restrung his bow. He glanced backward once. The white man followed.

A mile later they came to the lip of a bank above a medium-size creek. Tall cottonwoods lined the watercourse. A long-legged yearling mustang was tied to one of the trees with a lengthy tether. Beyond the colt the channel of the creek opened abruptly into the wide bottom of a major stream.

The Indian led down into the creek bed and to a hide-covered willow-pole teepee hidden in a copse of the cottonwoods. He threw back a large flap on the teepee to open up most of the interior. With a motion of his hand he invited Jubal inside.

With flint and steel Ghost Walker struck a spark to drop upon a dry piece of punk wood. The spark took life under his gentle coaxing breath and began to send up a tendril of smoke. Finely shredded bark was laid upon the glowing red coal. It took flame. Larger fuel was added.

Jubal stood close, watching the Indian's practiced hands build the fire. The man's back was to him. So easy to kill with knife or gun.

Ghost Walker turned, and as if reading Clason's thoughts, evaluated his new acquaintance. Neither spoke or moved, each probing the other's mind.

Jubal pulled his long skinning knife from its sheath, turned its butt toward the Indian and handed it to the bronze-skinned man. Then he turned his back and remained perfectly motionless.

Ghost Walker looked at the back of the white man. He was the first man Ghost Walker had spoken to in many moons. He badly missed Bird Flying and Old Pony Man. He had planned that upon his return to his village after his trial of strength and bravery, he never again would be separated from his people. Yet here he was an outcast. He must accept that, but oh, Great Spirit, it was terrible to be forever alone.

The thought of slaying the white man came and went and was but a momentary thing to the Arapaho. He already sensed a growing comradeship with the hairy-faced man. It had begun during those moments when each had stared at the other over faulty weapons. They had shared a unique experience of closeness to death and tested the courage of the other. It was hard to hate a brave man. Also Ghost Walker liked the easy laugh of the man, and he seemed to be a lone traveler like himself.

A minute passed, and a second one. Jubal waited for a third to flow by. He faced back to the Indian. The knife was on the ground and the man was regarding the blaze of the fire.

Clason retrieved his knife. "Now that we have settled that we're not going to kill each other, let's cook some of that backstrap meat. I haven't eaten since early yesterday."

They squatted in the shadow of the teepee. The meat, pierced by a green wooden rod and hanging over the fire, cooked to a golden brown. Its juices bubbled out to fall into the hot coals, to explode with little splutters of steam.

The men pulled their sharp knives and cut off the cooked brown surface strips of the meat and ate. Then as the exposed deeper portion of the meat also browned under the heat of the flames and coals, they started with their knives again.

As Jubal devoured the tasty flesh, he ranged his sight along the top of the steep banks of the creek. The fire was sending a small quantity of smoke rising in the calm air. The odors of fire and cooking meat were strong. Such signals of the presence of man could bring danger from a far distance.

On the point of land where the creek emptied out into the valley of the larger stream, three gray-white buffalo wolves were skylined. Motionless, they observed the men.

One of the wolves, a large male, leisurely stretched one hind leg and then the other. He looked down at a herd of a hundred or so buffalo that had come into sight on the bottomland of the large stream. The brown beasts, with side sweeps of their strong necks and heads, were plowing the snow aside to reach the buried prairie grass.

The male wolf threw one last flick of his eyes at the men, loped along the crest of the bank a dozen paces and then vanished over the brink. The others left, running effortlessly after him with powerful, limber muscles.

Soon they came back into view, gray splotches on the sparkling white snow near the herd. The buffalo lifted their heads and measured the approach of their ancient and constant enemies.

"They are brave wolves," said Ghost Walker. "Never do they grow hungry. Always they follow the buffalo and eat when they want."

"They take what they want and ask no one's approval," said Jubal. "Not a bad way to live."

Jubal was very quiet for a long time. Ghost Walker recognized some important judgment was being contemplated in the mind of his new acquaintance.

"They take what they want," Jubal repeated. "There is nothing that can harm them."

"Only a stronger and more fierce wolf," responded Ghost Walker.

"We should be like the wolf."

"How do you mean? You are as brave as the wolf now."

"I have lost all my provisions. My traps are gone. I have no horse. Yet over there a hundred miles, in Denver City, there are many men who have what I could use. They also have gold, much gold, I'm told."

The Arapaho waited. The white man had more to say.

"I have killed many men in the big war far to the east. I did it for no reason except someone told me to. Would it be any worse to kill a man for a horse or a bag of gold? Wouldn't something a man needed actually be more of a reason?"

"I would kill a Cheyenne for a cayuse. It would be better, though, to steal it and let the man live to find out how brave a thief I am. However, I do not think I would kill for this thing you call gold. Old Pony Man, my uncle, spoke to me of the white man's desire for the soft yellow metal. I do not understand why you want it."

"With gold a man can buy a horse, a woman or a rifle. Wouldn't you want those things?"

"Yes. I would like to give my people many rifles. We will fight the white man one day and only with the guns that shoot many times can we win."

"You can never win that war. There are too many of the white men. I have been to their big cities. They also have no fear of dying. I have seen hundreds, more than that, thousands, march straight into the rifle sights of other white men protected by earthworks and trees. They died. Damn, so many died. And the ones behind stepped upon the dead to go to their own deaths. I never could understand why."

Ghost Walker contemplated Jubal's statements. "That may be as you say. Still, my people must fight to keep their land."

"You are also brave men and do not fear dying. But you are few, and you never seem to organize more than a few hundred braves at any one time. You will lose."

The Arapaho watched the wolves move through the herd of buffalo, the large shaggy beasts pulling away a safe distance to let the predators pass. He spoke. "If a warrior cannot win, then he must take as many of his enemies with him into the spirit world as he can."

"There are great quantities of gold being dug from the mountains. You and I should take as much of those riches as we need. I would buy thousands of acres of land so no one could crowd me."

"I could buy many guns. Old Pony Man and the other men of my village must be armed for the battle. Even now there is some fighting."

"Then you are agreeable to helping me take the gold from the men of Denver City?"

"We must take much gold from the enemies of my people."

"Yes. We will take much gold."

"Then I will go with you and help you rob a thousand men if need be."

"Good!" exclaimed Jubal. "We will go close to Denver. You can make camp someplace where no one will see you. I will scout out someone leaving town with much gold and we will take it from him. What is your name?"

"Ghost Walker."

"Mine's Jubal Clason. Shake on our deal."

A small bud of worry was born deep inside Ghost Walker. Though this Jubal Clason was fearless, Old Pony Man had said white men had no honor. This man would kill his own kind. What would happen after they accumulated many pieces of gold? Would he kill Ghost Walker for the second half of the gold? Ghost Walker must be very cautious. If a man was to die, it must be Jubal Clason.

"Denver City is off there to the northwest. We can reach it

in two or three days," said Jubal. He hung his buffalo robe over a shoulder in preparation to leave.

"Any part of this teepee of yours you want to take?" asked Jubal.

"Only my sleeping robe and my fire starter. All else can be easily replaced. I will free my young cayuse and let him join with the wild ones. I have no time to train him now."

Ghost Walker stowed the remainder of the meat in the pouch and wrapped it inside his robe. It took him only a moment to release the mustang. Light-footed in freedom, the young horse left at a full run.

Jubal trotted off. Ghost Walker followed. He buried his doubt about the success of the venture in a far recess of his mind.

The wind died away as they traveled. By the time the sun reached its zenith, a balmy breeze was blowing, coming directly out of the south.

The snow turned to slush. Water started to course in the shallow drainages.

Clason and Ghost Walker splashed onward through the sloppy snow and water. The runners became wet to the waist. Neither slowed or spoke.

Jubal smiled as he contemplated the gold that would soon be his. The men that stood in his path were of no consequence. Men were easy to kill. A fifteen-cent bullet or a slash of his knife could do it.

CHAPTER 8

In the Elephant Corral the ten coal-oil lamps had been lit hours before. They hung, swinging gently by their slender chains, from the ceiling joists. The wavering flames within the glass globes cast a dim yellow light down upon the deserted monte, faro and blackjack betting boards.

Three of the poker tables were abandoned and covered with black dustcloths. At the last table several men and the night shift of saloon girls gathered around the two men playing poker. The noise of cards being shuffled, the metal clink of gold coins as bets were being made and the murmur of the players calling out the amount of the wagers sounded in the mostly empty gambling hall.

Luke Coldiron had been playing cards for more than two days. His back ached and there was a dull, throbbing beat behind his eyes. He was a damn fool for being here playing cards against Ed Chase, the ace of professional gamblers in the Colorado Territory.

The throng of people watching the game had grown tired of standing and had drawn chairs up close. Luke heard their combined breathing. The smell of the women's perfume mixed with the odor of the unwashed bodies of the men was strong and unpleasant.

Luke pulled the broad brim of his hat farther down in the front, throwing his entire face into shadow. He should have quit when he had bankrupted Sanderson. That was enough revenge for the blond man's cheating and Sanderson doing nothing to stop it.

For many hours now the pasteboards had flowed to Coldiron in a winning sequence like to a man possessed of all the love of Lady Luck. In that heady moment after taking Sanderson's last coin and still feeling anger at the professional for allowing a dishonest game, Luke had scooped up his golden winnings and moved to the next poker table.

Eleven hours later all the amateur players had fallen out of the game and Coldiron had won the bankroll of the professional. With mumbled curses the gambler tossed the deck of cards upon the playing surface, flopped a dust cloth over all and stomped off.

Luke piled the mound of winnings in his hat. He had enjoyed the intensity and concentration of the game and the confrontation of a worthy opponent. During the play there had been an odd sensation, a certain confidence that the cards would fall right for him to win.

Coldiron walked to the Charpiot Hotel, slept five hours and returned to the Elephant Corral. A third gambler surrendered his stake after eighteen hours of constant contest.

"I've lost all my poke," grumbled the gambler. "Damn your luck, Coldiron. Are you going to try to break every poker table? Even Ed Chase there?"

Luke raked in the wagers of the last hand and swiveled his sight to Chase, sitting at the adjoining table and idly playing solitaire as he waited for a challenger. He was a small, spare man with eyes sunk deeply under thick, wild eyebrows. He was about Luke's age. His hair was prematurely gray and combed back from a part in the middle of his head. His game was considered to be the most honest in all Denver.

"I make no boast," said Luke. "But I believe I will at least play a few hands with Ed. Is that all right, Ed?"

Chase had heard his name being mentioned and was watching. "Sure, Coldiron. I'd like that."

For the third time Luke transferred his growing pile of winnings to another table. He was richer by over eighteen thousand dollars. Methodically, he placed the many coins in neat piles.

"Cut for deal," said Chase. He shuffled and laid the deck in front of Luke.

* * *

By the evening of the second day, the snow had melted away and the prairie sod was soft and mushy under the moccasined feet of Ghost Walker and Jubal. They had run steadily, halting only to grab a quick bite of the meat of the buffalo calf and to sleep the dark hours of the night away. They both felt an unspoken urgency to get on with the deadly game that had been agreed upon.

Dusk was swiftly overtaking them from the east when the buildings of Denver emerged from out of the horizon. Jubal gestured ahead at the structures some three miles distant. Ghost Walker nodded that he had also spotted the town.

A few minutes later they approached one lone hill standing short above the flat plain. The Indian veered the course to climb to the brushy crown of the high ground.

"From here I can look down on the white men's village while I wait for you," said Ghost Walker.

"Good place to bivouac," acknowledged Jubal. "You can also see anybody coming from a long ways off in any direction."

"Bring me a very fine rifle. Then you can show me how to use it as well as you do."

"That'll take quite a spell of practice to be as crack a shot as me. But I'll bring you a rifle and cartridges. Stay close about, for we may need to leave in a hurry. Don't let anyone see you or there'll be a hundred riflemen out here after you."

Ghost Walker brought his hand down in a deprecating motion. "I will be as invisible as the wind. Yet like the powerful winds that sometimes strike out from the clouds, I may have slain several white men before you return."

"It makes no difference to me how many you kill. Keep any horses, guns or gold they may have. Just in case you don't come by horses, I'll steal us a couple and bring them back with me."

Jubal dropped down the side of the hill. His blood flowed faster as he contemplated the great quantity of gold that men in this town owned.

He knew there were two places where money was concentrated: banks and gambling halls. The latter was the more fitting to his plans. He wound his path through the dark streets of the town, glancing into the door of every saloon and card parlor he encountered. Finally, he entered the largest gambling establishment he had found. A sign over the porched entrance named it Denver House.

Among a score of other rifles, Jubal hung his Spencer on a wooden peg driven in the wall near the entrance. The first beer he drank quickly, the cool tanginess tickling his tongue and the liquid tumbling deliciously down his throat. The bartender poured a second upon Jubal's signal.

Noting that practically every person was at the far end of the long card room, Clason took his mug of beer and walked across the barroom. He glanced past the rough-sawn board partition that separated barroom from gambling area and looked over the rows of empty gaming boards to the two men playing cards.

The voice of an unseen man on the other side of the partition reached Jubal. ''Coldiron must've won twenty to twenty-five thousand dollars by now. I've never seen so much gold coin in one place before in my life.''

''Ferron was right, Lew,'' responded the second man. ''He said Coldiron was on a winning streak that nobody could stop. When we take his money, it sure is going to be a big haul for us.''

Lew chuckled. ''That Ferron sure does hate Coldiron.''

''Wouldn't you, too, if he had showed you the wrong end of a six-gun when you had been cheating?''

''Reckon so,'' said Lew. ''Roy, how do you suppose Ferron plans to take Coldiron's winnings?''

Jubal glided quickly closer to the partition, his moccasins as soundless as the pads of a mountain lion on the earthen floor. He did not want to miss the answer to that question.

''Won't be by standing straight up to him,'' said Roy. ''Coldiron's too fast for him. He'll bushwhack the fellow somewheres between Denver and his ranch.''

''That's the safest way, all right. To tell the plumb truth, from what I've heard about Coldiron, I don't hanker to take any unnecessary chances with him myself.''

''You worry too much. Ferron has never led us wrong. He always plays it smart.''

''Yeah. A long-range rifle shot sure does wonders to keep a man safe.''

"Things may not be all that easy. Coldiron may simply put his gold in the Kuntze Brothers Bank for safekeeping."

"I doubt that. His ranch is far south of here, much closer to Santa Fe. If he uses a bank, it'd be one there. Anyway, he'll take some gold with him. We'll take whatever he has on him."

"It doesn't make much difference whether or not he has gold. Ferron would go after him anyway just to kill him."

The men lapsed into silence and Jubal moved back to the bar for a third beer. He lifted it to his shaggy-haired face and drank. Those two men and a third named Ferron had staked out the rancher for a robbery and killing. Well, he wished them success. Then Ghost Walker and he would finish the game. At the thought of taking the gold from the thieves, Jubal laughed. Rob the robbers. He surely liked the idea.

The bartender came along the bar to talk to the man that laughed so pleasantly.

For two hours the higher cards had continued to flow to Luke. Ed Chase lost three thousand dollars. His countenance evidenced no more emotion than if the loss had been only a copper penny.

A man muttered in a whisper in the crowd. "By God, I believe Coldiron is really going to break every poker table in the Elephant."

A second low-toned voice answered. "Nobody has ever shut Chase's table down and nobody is going to. He's too good with the cards for that to happen."

"Coldiron just might do it."

"Luck can win in the short run, but going on three days is too long. A man's luck can turn between the dealing of one card and the next. And Ed Chase ain't like all the others. He's the very best. Been playing professional cards for over twenty years. I once saw him down to a hundred dollars. That was the first year he showed up here in Denver—'60, it was. He began to win and cleaned the other fellow. Took more'n ten thousand dollars off him."

"Skill will win in the end all right," said the first man. "What odds will you give on Chase?"

"Two to one Chase wins," the man answered in a confident voice.

"I'll take twenty dollars of that. Put forty dollars in a pocket by itself so it'll be there to pay me when you lose. I hope Coldiron's luck holds a few hours longer."

Within the hour the game became more even, with one man and then the other holding winning hands. Luke pondered the weaker trend of the cards.

As he picked up a hand dealt him, he felt the weariness like cotton in his brain. His zest for the game was gone. He ranged his view over the yawning hollow interior of the Elephant Corral.

The weather had warmed considerably during the past two days. The fires had been allowed to burn out in the heating stoves, and he smelled the dead, cold ashes. The press of expectant people, observing the change of the tenor of the cards, had drawn even closer. Their joint body heat radiated unwelcome warmth upon Luke.

Beyond the nearby crowd two men leaned talking against the partial partition separating the gambling hall from the barroom. A tall black-headed man in buckskin clothing stood close to the opposite side of the wall. He seemed to be listening, unseen by the other men, to what was being discussed.

As Ed Chase waited impatiently for Luke to bet, he covetously eyed the pile of gold in front of Coldiron. The man's luck had been durable, but now into the third day it was fading. Chase believed time was on his side. No hurry. Let more of that luck come to his side of the table.

Luke noted the first hint of daylight brightening the windows of the Elephant Corral. Another day was beginning. He tossed his hand of cards down and shoved back from the green felt-topped table.

"Chase, it's hot in here and I need to sleep the clock around a couple of times. The game's finished."

Chase riffled the cards with a rapid flipping sound. He repeated the action, his mind racing. "Coldiron, I've got five thousand dollars left that says your luck is gone and I can beat you. What say we bet that amount and look at each other's cards."

The crowd stirred. The man who had given two-to-one odds on Chase poked his partner with an elbow and whispered, "I'm feeling good, like I'm about to take your twenty dollars."

Coldiron spoke. "I don't care whose luck is better. The game is ended."

"Bet me!" demanded the gambler in a gruff voice.

"No," said Luke, his anger rising at the insistence of the man.

"All right, then, I'll show you anyway who can draw the best cards," declared Chase. He began to deal.

Luke did not look at the face of the falling cards. Instead, he watched the sunlight turn the front window of the Elephant Corral to gold.

Chase made a grunting sound. Luke glanced down at the cards. A nine-high straight lay before the gambler. A very good hand. He checked his own cards. Three aces and two jacks were spread upon the table. A lovely hand.

Chase swallowed and stretched his flat gambler's smile across his lips. "Guess your luck is still the strongest."

Luke's headache subsided slightly as he counted his money and placed it in a golden square. When he had finished, he spoke to Chase. "Luck can't be measured by a hand that has no money bet on it."

"I guess not," agreed Chase. "One day I'll take back the money you've won off me."

"Anytime I'm in town and you want to have a go at it, let me know."

"I'll do that." Chase stood and picked up his money. Without looking either left or right, he pushed through the people and chairs to the bar.

Luke called out to Teats. "You got a leather bag I can tote this loot in?"

"Sure. I'd be glad to give you one. Also, be glad to get rid of you. You're bad for business."

Luke roved his sight over the furnishings of the Elephant. "Maybe next time I'll play you. I'd like to own this place."

"You'll never make it. I never gamble with a man when his luck is running."

"Yep. That's all it was. Pure luck," said Luke. He lifted the pouch of gold. Now to sleep the day completely around. He walked past the tall man in buckskin watching him from the bar and went out into the sunlight of a new day.

*   *   *

Susan Penfold carried her bedroll and rifle down the carpeted stairway of the Charpiot Hotel and out onto the street. Where a small patch of lamplight from the window of the hotel lobby fell upon the wooden planking, she stopped and looked along the street. Night shadows still lingered beneath the porches of the buildings and in the narrow alleyways. There was a faint yellow blush in the eastern heavens, a harbinger of the sun soon to rise.

In the half-light of the street, her husband Dan and her younger brother Phil were stowing gear upon the three packhorses. All the riding animals were already saddled except for her gray gelding. A saddle for that mount had been placed on the edge of the sidewalk. Dan had not forgotten. She always wanted to tend her own horse.

A sweep of cold wind washed over her and continued up the street. She shivered at its touch and laid her bedroll and rifle down so she could button her heavy sheepskin coat. She knew her chill was not all from the wind. What she and the two men planned to do was very dangerous, probably foolhardy.

The three of them had found gold in a rugged, rocky canyon in the mountains. By working from daylight to dark every possible day for two years, they had accumulated seven hundred ounces of the precious metal. A small fortune to take back with them to Massachusetts.

However, finding and digging the gold, as difficult as that had been, might be the easiest part. Now the six-hundred-mile journey across the prairie to St. Joe through the snowy storms of November and December lay ahead. The Indians were out there waiting in ambush; already they had stopped the stages from daring to make their runs. Also, white men—thieves and killers—had attacked many travelers. Some of the victims had lived to struggle back to Denver to tell the story.

Susan and the two men had deliberately waited until winter had struck the prairie and mountains, dropping its first snow upon the land. The Indians would be gathered in their winter camps in the timbered breaks along the rivers and not in war parties stalking the paths east. The white renegades would have come in off the windy trails and taken up abodes in Denver.

It was time to begin the journey on their fast-stepping

horses. She drew a deep breath as she considered the danger that faced them during the next few weeks. She smelled the odor of mud in the street and the pungent scent of fresh horse droppings lying dense in the air. From the restaurant half a block away came the mutter of voices of people eating an early breakfast. For an instant there was the salty aroma of bacon frying. Beyond the eatery a horseman left the livery stable and came along the street. The rough town of Denver was stirring, coming alive around her.

A dog barked shrill, sharp yaps to the west. She turned that direction and saw the round winter moon lying on the jagged mountain horizon.

The land was stark and harsh. Yet she felt immensely exhilarated by being here. Dan had told her in one of their intimate, private conversations that she had more courage than either Phil or he. That was not true, for they both were brave men. But she smiled in remembrance.

Coldiron left the livery stable and, towing his packhorse, headed up the street toward the Charpiot Hotel. He passed the hitch rail tied full of horses in front of the restaurant. Inside, a man's voice called, "More coffee over here."

At the Charpiot Luke dismounted. The reins were dropped on the edge of the sidewalk to ground tie his mount. The well-trained animal would hold the packhorse from wandering off.

Luke saw the six horses in the street on his left. He cast a measuring eye over the two men with them. A small man wearing a sheepskin coat was standing looking at the mountains over the rooftops of the buildings. As Luke passed the figure to enter the hotel, the person's face came more into view. The features were those of a woman, finely chiseled, with large eyes and a generous mouth upon which played a pleasant smile. Altogether a charming sight.

Beneath a man's wide-brimmed hat pulled low, her dark hair was pulled tightly back and tied with a rawhide band. She wore a man's cord trousers and boots. From a distance, she could pass as a male. Up close like this, there was nothing mannish about her.

Savoring the agreeable glow he always felt when seeing a pretty woman, Luke entered the hotel to retrieve his gold from the safe. He wanted to be far down the trail home before daylight.

"Ready to leave, Susan?" asked Dan.

"Yes. Just as soon as I get my horse saddled." She lifted up the saddle and stepped down into the mud of the street beside the gray gelding. With a strong pull of her arms, she hoisted the saddle into place on the muscular back. The cinch was quickly tightened.

Susan fastened the bedroll behind the seat with leather thongs. She returned to the sidewalk and bent to pick up her rifle.

Luke came out of the Charpiot Hotel carrying his bag of gold hanging over a shoulder. He stepped to the side away from the door, halted, and warily scanned the street. Denver had many thieves, drifters and scoundrels. There was little law to control them. And no law beyond the borders of the town.

He had considered depositing the gold in the vault of the Kuntze Brothers bank. However, in these uncertain times of civil conflict, with parts of the country fighting each other and local law enforcement sadly weakened, what bank could really insure the safety of its patrons' funds. Best a wise man protect his own wealth.

On the edge of the sidewalk Susan straightened up with the rifle in her hands. She pivoted around intending to go to her horse. The barrel of the weapon made a swift arc through the air. The open end of the muzzle swung to point directly at a man near the door of the hotel.

Faster than she could imagine, the man leaped from in front of the gun, flipped the tail of his coat out of the way and drew his six-gun. The expression upon his face was deadly, the intent to kill her plain.

Susan cried out a short, startled note at his sudden action. Her eyes widened to circles of astonishment.

The momentum of the rifle continued its swing. The bore of the barrel moved past Coldiron. He read the lack of menace in the woman. He struggled to stop the movement of his finger, a finger that had from long practice begun to press the trigger of his pistol the instant it cleared the holster. At the last fraction of time he stopped himself from firing.

"God!" exclaimed Coldiron. His breath sucked in and he

gave an involuntary jerk of disbelief at how near he had come to shooting the woman. There was a tremble in his hand as he slid the six-gun back into its holster.

"Damnation, woman!" Luke said angrily. "Be careful where you point that thing."

"I—I'm sorry," stammered Susan. "I didn't know you were there."

Coldiron realized his action was not justified. She had made an innocent mistake. His anger deflated. He grinned ruefully into the remorseful eyes of the woman. "I guess it's not all your fault. I was wound up a little tight myself."

He saw the two men circling hastily around the horses to come to the woman's aid. Their hands were on their pistols. They must think he was threatening her. "No harm done, fellows," Coldiron called to them. "I took some alarm when she accidentally aimed her rifle in my direction."

The older of the two men was about to say something when Luke looked back at the woman. "I'm sorry for my cussing." He stepped swiftly across the sidewalk, and hoisted up the pouch of gold to slide it into one of the packs on the horse. Without looking again at the three people, now grouped together and watching him, he mounted and left at a fast lope.

"You okay, Susan?" Dan asked.

"Yes," responded the woman, observing the outline of the man and his horse growing indistinct as he drew away in the diffused grayness of the morning dawn. She still felt his presence, like a strong wind primed to do fierce, savage things. "It was a foolish thing. I really am the one that caused it. Let's hurry and go."

They mounted and, towing the three packhorses, made their way north along the muddy street.

CHAPTER 9

Coldiron let his rested and willing horses run through the mild November morning. They drummed across the hard land and splashed the shallow pools of snow-melt water glowing dull silver under the slanting rays of the early sunlight.

Without being guided, the horses moved south along the base of the mountains toward the New Mexico Territory. They followed exactly the route used coming to Denver. Some of the previously made tracks, though distorted and eroded by the melting of the heavy snowfall, were still visible in the dirt.

To the east of Luke, the brown prairie-grass plain stretched to the far, flat horizon. On the opposite hand, looming high above, the snow crowns of the tall Rockies shined sparkling white against the strong blue sky.

Several times he halted on a higher ridgeline and warily examined his back trail for riders. A lone man traveling with thousands of dollars in gold would be a tempting target for the many bandits that headquartered in Denver.

Each time he checked to the rear, the low, grass-covered hills lay empty and he hurried onward. He meant to stay ahead of any possible outlaws and if a battle was to be fought, select the ground for it himself.

The treeless plain near Denver was left behind and Luke entered low, rolling hills with stunted juniper. An hour later he had traversed the hills and come down onto level land. The horses picked up the pace.

By late morning he was twenty miles from Denver. He was out of the range of the meat hunters and began to see game. A small herd of buffalo watched him from a distance. Farther away a couple dozen elk grazed the frostbitten grass. A high-flying wedge of geese moved south close to the forested flanks of the mountains. Their wings seemed to scrape the very tops of the trees.

Coldiron began to relax. The horses slowed to a walk.

His course brought him to a vertical walled ravine some fifty feet deep and twice that wide thrusting out from the mouth of a steep mountain stream. In the sandy bottom flowed a moderate-size creek. Gradually, in a mile stretch the ravine swerved to the southeast.

The impassable barrier had forced all travelers—men and wild animals—to detour around. Close to the edge of the obstacle the stomping hard hooves of the deer and elk, but mostly the great buffalo, had hollowed out a deeply worn trail as broad as a tall man and nearly two feet deep.

Coldiron veered off on the much used game trail. As he continued, the depth of the nearby gully slowly shallowed to five or six feet. On the far side the land became blanketed with large juniper.

Luke evaluated the dense stand of trees that elbowed each other for space and soil to grow in. With the ravine funneling game past at a short rifle range, a man hidden in the trees could easily kill an animal. Or could kill a man who would alter his course to pass the obstruction.

If outlaws had in some manner outridden him and gotten ahead, this was an ideal place for a surprise attack. Also, an enemy could correctly assume he would return home on a familiar route. By asking a few discreet questions of Kerr, the horse trader, or someone else who knew him, bandits could have left anytime before him and now be lying in wait.

Luke cursed himself for his laxness. He could be under the guns of bushwhackers at this very moment. He raked his mount with spurs. The powerful beast lunged ahead on the ancient game trail.

"Ferron, do you see anything?" asked Lew, lying on the ground with his hat over his face.

"Damn it, keep quiet. I'll tell you when he comes,"

growled the blond man. He sat leaning against the trunk of a
juniper and looking out through the limbs. The trail beside
the ravine could be seen for more than a mile.

The three of them had been in this exact location since the
afternoon of the day before. When Coldiron stopped playing
cards, Lew and Roy had reported it to Ferron. He had already
developed his scheme to rob the rancher, and they had immediately packed enough supplies to last a week and left Denver. To insure they made no sign on the trail he believed
Coldiron would use, Ferron guided a parallel course farther
east on the prairie.

Something moved on the trail, a black figure at a range of
about half a mile. It was large enough to be a buffalo.

The object divided into two horses. A man rode one.

"He is coming," said Ferron. "Wake Roy."

Lew poked Roy with the toe of his boot. "Come alive. But
keep quiet. We're going to have some target practice in a
minute."

The third man rose up blinking. " 'Bout time. I don't want
to spend another night out here. I want to get back to Denver
and find someone to help me warm my bed."

Ferron cut in. "Check the loads in your rifles. We want to
do this right."

Both men levered the action of their weapons to shove
brass cartridges into the firing chambers.

"Here's how we will do it," said Ferron. "You two kill
Coldiron's packhorse. That's where the gold will most likely
be. I'll shoot Coldiron. I owe him a hot chunk of lead in the
gut. Don't quit firing until both the horses are dead. That's
just in case the gold is on the second horse. Now get ready.
Find a place where you can see him good but can't be seen."

The two men went to the right and began to peer through
the stiff green needles of the juniper. Lew spoke. "About
three hundred yards. His horses are only walking. This'll be
easy shooting."

"Ferron, I like your way of finding gold," chuckled Roy
in a whisper. "In someone's pocket already dug and washed."

"When he gets exactly opposite us, I'll give the word and
we'll shoot," Ferron said. He watched the man on the lead
horse. You son of a bitch, soon you'll be dead.

"Aim your rifles, directed the gang leader, and centered the sights of his gun upon Luke.

At that instant of time, for a reason the outlaw leader could not determine, the rider spurred his mount.

"Fire!" yelled Ferron, and shot at the rapidly accelerating figure.

Three rifles crashed out in a crescendo of explosions.

Luke's packhorse had maintained station on the riding horse, holding slack in the lead rope to prevent rough jerks on its neck. Now as Luke's mount leaped forward, the packhorse was still walking. The first shot from Lew's gun slammed the animal down to the ground.

Ferron's slug missed Coldiron, passing behind. The outlaw hastily levered in another round and swung the barrel to lead the target.

The lead rope fastened to the one thousand pounds of dead horse was yanked taut as Luke's steed hit the end of the slack. The cinch of the saddle snapped in two. Man and saddle flew from the back of the horse.

As Luke fell, he saw the rocky trail flying up to hit him. His head slammed a stone. The world spun out of focus and plunged into complete darkness.

A throbbing, brain-tearing pain came to life in his head as consciousness rushed back. The pain picked up the beat of his heart, roaring with excruciating agony with each pulse of his blood. He was dizzy and felt like vomiting. He thought his skull was broken.

Ever so gently, he rolled his head first to one side and then the other. He lay on his back crossways of the buffalo trail beside his saddle. The dead packhorse was on the right, the body of his mount on the left.

The shots had come from the juniper on the west side of the arroyo. Could the gunmen see him from there? He looked backward over his head. Above the upward curve of the edge of the trail, the top half of the juniper could be seen. He could not rise more than an inch or so or he would be within the sights of the bushwhackers' rifles. His feet were extended onto the far side of the trail and were probably within view now.

His hand carefully snaked out for the rifle in the scabbard beneath the saddle. He eased the long-barreled gun free and dragged it to him. Holding it pressed close to his stomach, he worked the lever to slide in a cartridge. The gunmen would soon come and the shooting would start again. This time he intended to do his share.

Then he waited, his head cocked to pick up the slightest sound and his nose constantly testing the air for the sour, stale odor of unwashed human bodies.

Thick black clouds pushed in to mask the blue of the sky. Now and then, through small holes in the masses of moisture, Coldiron caught a glimpse of the sun marching to its zenith and beginning its long curving fall toward the western horizon.

A vulture sailed in at a thousand-foot elevation and started to circle the still forms of the man and horses on the ground. Luke regarded the buzzard, its wings set and using all its skill to ride the feeble updrafts to maintain its height. I'm not yours yet. With a whole lot of luck I may give you someone else to feed on.

A puff of wind rattled the dry grass on the border of the trail. Coldiron almost sat up before he identified the sound and caught himself. He mustn't move. Let them think him dead or badly wounded and come to him.

The sun sank behind the mountains, and dark shadows crawled into the trench of the buffalo trail with Coldiron. He was stiff beyond measure. Not once had he dared move his feet. When they did come sneaking up on him, he most likely could not rise to fight them.

How would he attack a man in a situation such as his? If there was more than one to do the job, then post a man on high ground to watch for movement and kill if the prey stirred. The others could come stalking quietly and fire down into the trench of the trail at the victim.

The patience of the outlaws must be very long or they would have come by now. The patience of the buzzard was less, for it had ceased its circular orbit above and was gliding away.

Luke tightened his finger on the trigger of the rifle. Was the buzzard leaving because of the growing dimness, or had it seen life, movement? Had the gunmen left the cover of juniper and would they now be in the open? Were they finally coming? Every nerve was focused and strained to detect the approach of his enemies.

Luke flopped over onto his stomach and arched the trunk of his body up so he could see out of the hollow of the trail. He thrust his rifle out to a shooting position.

A man stood on the far bank of the ravine. At the appearance of Coldiron's head, the outlaw jerked his rifle up.

Too slow. Coldiron shot him through the chest.

Luke tried to stand; his legs refused to support him. He fell. He attempted to stand again and failed. He heard noises under the lip of the ravine. There was no cover there, he recalled quickly. He had to kill whoever it was before they could get into hiding.

He clambered shakily to his feet, and holding a tight rein on the pain in his head, staggered out of the trail and looked down. Two men raced toward some brush cover in the shallower end of the stream channel. Luke recognized the blond-haired card cheat of the Elephant Corral.

I might have known it would be you, thought Coldiron. He raised his rifle and broke the man's spine. Immediately, Luke shot the second man.

Hastily, he threw himself back into the hollow of the trail. With only his eyes showing, he raked the juniper and the land all around for more gunmen.

Nothing stirred in the gloom of the old day. A horse nickered somewhere at a distance back in the juniper. Had it sensed its master's death?

An hour passed. Darkness formed in the bottoms of swales and gullies and flowed out to blanket the land. He must find the horses of the bandits before it got too black to see.

Cautiously, he rose to his knees. He saw no danger, heard nothing. All his enemies must be dead. He stood erect and climbed up on the ridge of earth separating the trail from the vertical wall of the creek bank.

A stabbing, searing pain slugged him in the back. He heard the crack of the powerful rifle and a shrill war cry. Just before he lost consciousness and tumbled head first down into the bottom of the ravine.

"Damn good shooting for a beginner and in weak light, too," Jubal Clason told Ghost Walker. "You hit him dead center. I saw the dust fly from his shirt."

"Too bad he had to die, for he was a brave fighter,"

responded the Indian. "Even wounded he killed those three thieves."

"Yeah, I figured we'd have to do that. But because he was tough, that's why he had to be shot. Now it's done and the gold is ours. Let's go get it."

Jubal and Ghost Walker came out of the juniper not two hundred feet from where Ferron and his cohorts had lain in ambush. Dropping into the bottom of the ravine, they crossed the sandy bottom to the crumpled and motionless body of the rancher.

They stared down at the slack figure. Blood was thick and crusted on Coldiron's head. A large quantity of fresh blood soaked his shirt. His mouth hung open, half full of sand. His chest did not move.

"He's not breathing. He's dead," said Clason. He stopped and ran his hands over Luke's waist. "No money belt here. All of his gold must be on one of the horses. I'll take his pistol, for he'll not be needing it anymore."

Luke's mind was full of bursting stars and spinning pin-wheels of bright light. He could not breathe and he knew he would soon be dead. The battered skull and the shock of the bullet wound held him in a web of total weakness. No muscle could move.

Seconds were as minutes as he strove to force his crippled body to function, to survive. He never heard the two men talking nor did he feel the searching hands.

Jubal and Ghost Walker were busily counting Coldiron's gold when he first noted a tiny zone of control in a corner of his stunned brain. Other sections of his mind began to work. His chest heaved spasmodically with breath. His weakly fluttering heart gained energy and the red tide of life began to flow in his veins. He felt the hot blood of hate and revenge pumping strength into him. He would not die. He would make some other man die.

He lay very still and rested.

After a while he began to shiver with cold. With a mighty effort, he managed to sit up. All about him was a dark November night. A crisp, cold wind droned down the arroyo. The temperature was dropping rapidly.

He placed his hands on the ground and tried to rise. He

could not even lift his hips. Unless he found protection, he would freeze to death before morning.

He wished for his coat or a blanket. They were an impossible distance away, even if they were still in his pack. With his hands he laboriously clawed a shallow trench in the sandy soil close beside him. He rolled into it and raked the loose earth in on top of him, covering himself to his chin.

Warmth came back little by little as his body warmed the soil. Worried how badly he was bleeding, Luke drifted off into a pain-filled sleep.

He awoke to a cold, sullen day. The gray clouds had lowered and hung close above the earth. His pain had subsided to a dull ache.

He sat up, the dirt falling away. Giddiness stopped his progress for a minute, then he managed to get to his knees. Again he waited for a clear head and strength to rebuild. Finally, he stood erect on wobbly legs and made his way to the stream.

Rims of ice bordered the banks. His teeth ached as he drank deeply of the water that had come down from the snow of the mountains.

Tenderly, he walked down the arroyo and climbed out where the bank was low. Vultures were at the horses, eating the flesh not covered by the saddle or packs. At his appearance the birds ran awkwardly away from their feast, flapping long black wings until they could get airbore with their heavy, gluttonous bellies.

His supplies were scattered around as if someone had picked through them. He could not find rifle or pistol. There were tracks of two men, both wearing moccasins. Remembering the war cry, Luke reasoned one could be an Indian. Perhaps both. One day he hoped to find out who they were, just before he killed them.

He discovered a packet of dried apples and chewed on them as he considered his predicament. His head appeared much improved. The wound in his back did not seem to be deep and there was no fresh blood. A good sign. He just might live if he could find a gun and a horse.

He moved back toward the ravine and the bodies of the outlaws. Maybe the men that had shot him had not taken all the weapons from the corpses.

He felt in his pockets as he walked. One thin five-dollar gold piece was in the corner of a front pocket. That was all that remained of the small fortune he had carried.

Luke found no rifles. A much abused six-gun with broken grips was on one of the bodies. Seemed someone did not believe it worth taking, at least not when he had thousands of dollars in gold. Luke removed the cartridge belt and holster from the dead man and buckled it about his own waist. To his surprise the action of the weapon was tight and worked smoothly in his hands. It was a very serviceable gun.

He began to circle the ambush site for sign that would help him interpret what had happened and came upon the tracks of three men. Then the prints of two more. He traced both sets to their hiding places. The groups had not been together and Luke could not decipher that. Judging from the location of their hiding places, he must have shot the men in the group of three. Two men had left to the east with five horses.

He filled a gallon canteen with water and selected a quantity of food from the remnants of his supplies. During his long-ago beaver-trapping days, Coldiron had acquired the habit of using a buffalo robe for winter sleeping. He saw the skin lying on the ground and added it to his heap of salvaged goods.

One of the packs was removed from the packhorse, and with some leather straps he made it into a large satchel. He stowed his supplies in the container and hung it over his shoulder. His sleeping robe went over the other shoulder. He trudged off walking upon the very tracks left by the two bushwhackers that had shot him from hiding and left him for dead.

CHAPTER 10

Susan and the two men rode hard. They pressed north, alternately galloping and walking their horses through the tall prairie grass. Denver sank into the land lying under the mountains and was lost miles behind.

"We've come far enough," said Dan. "Anyone who saw us leave will think we're heading out to pan for gold in the streams emptying onto the plains. No one will suspect we are carrying forty pounds of gold and are going home." He smiled at both his companions and angled his mount to lead a course due east.

In the afternoon thick clouds overran the riders and obscured the sky. The wind picked up and the grayish brown grass stretching to the flat, far-flung horizon began to whip and toss in long rolling waves.

To Susan the horses seemed to be wading through a shallow sea from which an enemy could spring up from hiding at any instant and fire guns at them or shoot sharp arrows from war bows. She remembered how utterly defenseless she had been when the cowboy in Denver had suddenly appeared and drew his six-gun to threaten her. The violence of that moment had destroyed her simple concept of how she would challenge the danger ahead.

She had learned that a fraction of a second could mean the difference between life and death. She pulled her rifle from its scabbard and held it ready in her hands.

Dan saw his wife arm herself. He examined her sensitive

features. She was worried, and it showed in the tiny crow's feet at the corners of her eyes. Yet there was a defiant cock to her head.

He nodded his understanding at her. She was one very brave woman. "We'll make it. If we do get into trouble, shoot to kill and shoot fast."

Susan looked into his sober eyes. "None of us have killed a man. I hope we never have to. But if it becomes necessary, I guess we are all capable of it."

"Right you are, sis," Phil called out above the sound of the thud of horses' hooves. "We must stay alert and spot any Indians before they see us."

"With all the gold we have, white men may be the most likely source of trouble," said Dan. "There are probably many outlaws out here just waiting for travelers like us."

Susan knew it was a dangerous, reckless thing they were doing. It had also been a rash endeavor to leave their safe home in Massachusetts to go to Colorado in search of gold. However, they found their gold and with arduous labor had torn the treasure from the mountains.

The storms and bone-chilling cold of that high land was past them. Now a swift dash across the prairie to St. Joe, and from there all that remained was a leisurely train ride the rest of the way home.

"Let's pick up the pace," said Dan. They kicked the horses into a ground-devouring lope.

Susan matched her speed to Dan's. Vigilantly, her eyes scouted the terrain, sweeping over the dead grass flicking and rippling in the wind. This was a vast, wild land preparing for winter. A perilous land they were committed to cross. Or die trying.

They rode the gloomy day into the cloudy dusk of evening.

The pack of lean gray wolves heard the noise of heavy animals approaching and surged up from the grass where they had lain resting. Their keen, untamed eyes instantly found the aliens trespassing in their domain. With tails stuck rigidly out and quivering behind them and every hair radiating infinite suspicion, the powerful hunting beasts watched the three humans on the horses. The wind was to them and they lifted their noses to test the heavy scent of man and woman.

Susan and the men pulled to a fast halt and stared back at the four adult wolves and four mostly grown pups. "Buffalo wolves," said Phil. "There must be a herd of buffalo somewhere near here."

At the sound of Phil's voice the wolves came out of their frozen stance and with a deceptive swiftness moved away, to fade into the shadow-filled grass.

"The wolves seemed not to have been bothered until we got here," said Susan. "That may mean no other people are around. It's nearly dark, so let's camp here."

"There's a gully just over there," said Dan, pointing. "Let's camp down in the bottom of it and we'll be out of the wind and out of sight of anybody up here on top."

They guided the horses down a buffalo trail beaten into the bank of the wash and rode along a winding ribbon of water flowing in the creek bed. Where the bottom widened and a quarter acre of grass grew, Dan called a stop. They climbed stiffly from their mounts.

Dan spoke. "The horses must be allowed enough time to feed. I'll stake them out and then go back up and keep lookout on the prairie until it is dark."

"Okay," said Phil. "I'll string a picket rope between those bushes. We can tie the horses there after they graze a couple of hours. Close to us there'll be less of a chance someone can slip up and steal them without us knowing it."

The packs and saddles were unfastened and placed together near one wall of the gully. Susan started a small fire. She knew the growing darkness would hide the smoke and that the light from the flames could not be seen above the bank. Speedily, she cooked a warm meal and immediately piled dirt over the burning embers of the fire.

"Food is ready," Susan called up to her husband.

"Nothing to be seen up here," responded Dan. He dropped down into the bottom and made his way through the night shadows to squat beside Susan and Phil.

"Here's your food," said Susan and passed him a tin plate heaped high and a full cup of coffee. They sat together and silently ate.

"We've made a lot of distance today," Dan spoke from the gloom. "Too bad part of it had to be in a direction out of our way. Still, we are headed right now. I doubt we'll be able to travel this far in one day very often.''

''Even if we are stormed on, we can make it to St. Joe in a month or thereabouts,'' Phil said.

''We must always be very watchful,'' said Susan. A nagging uneasiness pressed upon her. She sensed an impending loss of something very valuable to her. She watched the two men.

''Don't worry, sis. I got a feeling we'll all come out safe and sound,'' said Phil. He stood up. ''I'll go get the horses and bring them in before it gets completely dark.'' He left soundlessly on the grass.

Susan washed the utensils in the stream and stowed them away in the packs. After finishing she sat and listened to the soft noises of the prairie above the bank.

Phil returned and tethered the mounts to the short picket rope. ''They didn't get enough to eat. Tomorrow we must stop earlier. We want them always to be in good condition so they can outrun anything that tries to catch us.''

''One of us must stay awake and be on guard at all times during the night,'' said Dan. ''Who wants the first watch?''

''I'll take it,'' volunteered Susan. ''I'm tired, but not sleepy.''

''All right,'' agreed Dan. ''Keep your guns handy and sleep light. Don't shout out if something goes wrong. Just call out in a whisper. We'll hear.''

Susan took her blankets and spread them where she could lean against the bank and also touch the picket rope. She placed her rifle across her knees and pulled one of the coverings up around her shoulders.

Beneath the heavy clouds of the sky the darkness thickened and congealed to an impenetrable black mass. The wind gained in strength and poked down into the wash to swish the grass in a dry rustling.

Without the stars to see, the passage of time was unmeasurable to Susan. Now and then she felt her way along the picket line and checked the horses. Their friendly noses sniffed at her as she passed. Then, reseated, she listened intently, questing with her ears through the noises of the night for sounds that should not be there.

A whisper worked its way out of the wall of darkness.

"Susan, are you going to keep watch until daylight?" asked Dan.

"Is my watch up?"

"Must be, for I feel like I've slept for a long time."

"Then it is all yours," replied Susan. For the first time she felt the full weight of her exhaustion. She lay down in all her clothes, tugged both blankets snugly about her and fell asleep.

The sun did not shine the next day. The morning came sullen and late. In the afternoon rain leaked in a fine, cold drizzle from the dreary gray overcast. It stopped a couple of hours before dark. Susan talked little during the day and the men seemed unusually quiet.

They made camp early and where the grass was tall and plentiful. No attempt was made to build a fire with the damp buffalo chips and grass. A tarpaulin shelter was rigged. They unrolled their beds beneath it to be protected during the night from the threatening rain clouds.

Cloud Woman dipped her hairbrush into the paste of the black pigment and painted upon the soft buckskin shirt. The garment was for her husband Fast Running, so she made the design bold and strong like him. Her own shirt of matching colors—yellow, red and black—was already finished and stowed in her personal clothing pouch.

All summer they had lived with her people in the Shining Mountains. Now in three days' travel, they would reach the village of Fast Running. For that arrival their clothing should be of the very best. Fast Running must always be proud of the skill of his woman.

Their night camp was on the prairie two days from the mountains. It was located in the center of a shallow, saucer-shaped depression of twenty acres or so where the limestone rock of the earth's crust had been leached away by countless rainstorms. A fire of buffalo chips burned with a smoldering, smoky flame in front of a small hide teepee.

Fast Running sat beside the fire. His arrows lay drying in the warmth of the blaze. The drizzle that had fallen earlier in the day had wet the wooden shafts and matted the feather fletchings.

Periodically, he would pick up an arrow, sight down its length and, if needed, bend it gently in his hands to straighten it truly. The feathers were pressed between his fingers to the proper shape for accurate flight.

As he worked, Fast Running watched the lovely Cloud Woman paint upon the shirt. The skill of her eye and hand amazed him. A most beautiful object was being created before him.

Three narrow bands of alternating red squares and yellow triangles ran around the bottom of the shirt. A thin strip of prime ermine fur, sewn with stitching so fine that it could not be seen, crossed the top just below the ridge of the shoulders. Within the wide zone between the decorations, she had painted in black the images of animals he had slain.

Using heavy strokes, or maybe only a whisper of pigment, she brought to life under her brush elk, antelope and many other creatures. Vibrant figures with powerful muscles and antlers or horns seemed ready to spring from the garment so he could slay them.

Some showed an arrow or lance embedded in their flesh. In these beasts she had somehow produced a posture and contortion of form to manifest great pain.

She had made her own shirt with a more subdued pattern. The painted design on the lower border and the ermine fur strip at the top were a third smaller than on Fast Running's garment. In the middle space she had produced several wondrous landscapes, her remembrances of the mountain valleys they had wandered in during the summer months.

Fast Running knew he was witnessing a very rare talent. He was immensely pleased Cloud Woman kept his teepee.

Fast Running picked up his bow and arrows and stood erect. Glancing briefly at his black mustang, Cloud Woman's roan mare and the packhorse grazing the grass nearby, he walked up the slight incline toward the lip of the basin. Cloud Woman and he were in a remote land controlled by their people, the Cheyenne, but seldom used by them. There should be little danger from enemies. Even so, he wanted to see out over the great flat plain one more time before night closed them in.

Close overhead, low hanging clouds drove south under the pressure of a steady wind. Both to the north and west, streaks of rain leaked from their swollen bottoms.

In the gloom of the late day the gray hue of the prairie

grass reminded him of a war pony he once owned. It had been a brave animal, killed by an Arapaho lance in a battle three years past.

He reached the surface of the plain. His keen vision went first to the sun's rising place, in the direction where lay his people's village. Already the sky and land had fused into one wide black horizon for the night had already arrived there.

He rotated to the south, eyes inspecting the terrain. Two riders leading three horses were coming directly at him at a brisk trot.

Fast Running threw himself to the ground. In his one brief glimpse, he saw there was one white man and one Indian, or two Indians with one in white man's clothing. Like hunting dogs, they were trailing the scent of his fire that floated downwind.

Some instinct told Fast Running these men were foes. And who else would come to a strange camp so late in the evening.

Fast Running scrabbled back below the plain where he could not be seen by the riders, sprang to his heels and raced to the horses.

"Cloud Woman, two men are coming. I think they could intend to harm us. Hurry and saddle your cayuse and run him in that direction toward our village." Fast Running stabbed a hand to the east. "The men will not be able to find you in the night."

Cloud Woman grabbed her buffalo-hide saddle, flung it upon the back of her mare and jerked the leather cinch tight. Fast Running jumped astride his strong war pony and spun him on his heels to view Cloud Woman. She was hastily cramming articles into her carrying bag.

"Woman, there is no time for that. Let the rest go and get out of here," commanded Fast Running.

"But we have many valuable things here."

"I want you safe above all else. Get on your cayuse and ride. If there is no battle, I will bring our belongings and catch up with you. Do not try to find me if we get separated. Go to my father's lodge. I will meet you there if I do not find you before that."

Cloud Woman fastened her partially filled pouch to the horse and hurriedly pulled herself up into the saddle. One

cutting lash of her rawhide whip sent the mare running full
tilt. Clods of damp earth flew from under the driving hooves.

Fast Running reined his black horse to face in the direction
the strange men would come from. He fitted an arrow on the
string of his bow. In this his homeland he would not run and
hide. He was not afraid of two men.

Behind him Cloud Woman dragged her mount to a halt
beyond the range of any arrow that might be shot in a battle.
She would be safe here in the deepening shadows and she
wanted to remain near Fast Running as long as possible.

Jubal and Ghost Walker came up to the verge of the basin
and, halting, looked ahead. At a range of two hundred yards,
an Indian warrior on a big black horse faced them.

"It's not a white man," said Clason. "He'll not have any
gold."

"Cheyenne. Just as I thought we probably would find,"
Ghost Walker said. "Most white men do not use the dried
buffalo droppings as fuel for their fires. I could smell the
buffalo odor in the smoke."

"He doesn't seem to be afraid of us," replied Clason,
regarding the calm countenance of Fast Running.

"Because he did not run into the darkness where we could
not see him, he will lose his life."

Seeing the bow in the Cheyenne's hand, Jubal spoke to the
Arapaho. "You have a natural skill for shooting the rifle.
You could kill him from here while still out of bow range."

"No. I will fight him with the same weapons he has."

"You have the advantage of him. Why gamble on an even
fight? A man could get wounded and be laid up for days. Or
he could plainly get killed."

Ghost Walker regarded Clason, masking his disdain for the
white man's inability to understand. "When I have killed the
Cheyenne with an arrow, the honor to me of winning will be
much greater." He unfastened his bow from behind the saddle
and, bracing it against the withers of the horse, strung it. He
placed the strap of his quiver of arrows over his head and one
shoulder. A feathered shaft was selected and nocked.

Fast Running saw the Arapaho warrior arming himself. He
must prepare himself for the battle. He tucked his bow and
arrow temporarily under a leg while he tied a length of

rawhide into a handful of the thick mane of his horse. Then
he fastened the free end to a thong on his buckskin jacket.
Next he extracted a leather strap from his pack and, bending
down with it, encircled the front leg of his mount, pulled both
ends up and tied them together. The straps reached nearly to
the top of the horse's back.

Removing his right foot from the stirrup, Fast Running
inserted it through the loop of leather. He was ready. With
one movement, he could throw himself down to hang suspended along the side of the horse. The full thickness of the
animal's body would shield him.

Observing what the Cheyenne was doing, Ghost Walker
spoke to Clason. "I wish I had my war pony or buffalo
hunter to ride."

"Yeah. You're going to have to sit up on top and be an
easy target. But you can still use your rifle."

"It is almost dark and I will be moving fast. I will be
safe." He rode toward his opponent.

"You would be a hell of a lot smarter to give the Cheyenne
a rifle and tell him to go and shoot white men," Jubal called
after Ghost Walker.

The Arapaho heard Clason's voice, but with all his attention focused on the Cheyenne, the meaning of the statement
was not understood.

Fast Running signaled his cayuse and it moved forward.
Any Arapaho trespassing on Cheyenne land must be slain.
The white man would be next.

The ponies broke into a run straight for each other. The
gap closed swiftly.

Fast Running lowered himself to hang on the side of his
steed. Only one lower leg and a foot, arched over the back of
the mount, was exposed to the enemies' arrows. He bent the
bow and sighted under the muscular black neck of his horse.

Jubal watched the two Indians charging upon each other.
He saw the Cheyenne fall from view. The Arapaho lay flat on
the back of his horse. As they hurtled past with not more than
twenty feet separating them, each man let loose his arrow.

The flight of Ghost Walker's arrow was not seen by Jubal.
The Cheyenne's arrow clipped off a lock of Ghost Walker's
long, blowing hair. The severed black strands flared like an
exploding chunk of darker night, and dropped to the ground.

Fast Running swung erect on the back of his steed and reined his cayuse back toward the Arapaho. As he turned, he cast one quick glance at the white man. The man was merely sitting his horse and watching.

Clason saw the men kick their mounts into a run and draw a second arrow. Ghost Walker should kill his foe's horse. Then kill the man when he was in view. However, Ghost Walker would not harm the horse unless by accident.

Clason needed the Arapaho uninjured. The Indian was tough and soon would be an expert rifleman. The two of them working together could protect each other and make an excellent pair of robbers. The fight should be ended now.

With one smooth movement, Clason yanked his Spencer from its scabbard, centered it on the back of the Cheyenne and fired. The man was slammed forward onto the neck of his pony. He clung there for two lunges of his mount, then slid sideways to be suspended by his foot in the leather loop and by his jacket tied to the horse's mane. His limp foot came free, and he was dragged by his jacket, bumping and bouncing along the ground.

The well-trained cayuse, sensing the strangeness of its master's position, came to a stop. It twisted to sniff at the body and did not like the smell of death. It whinnied loudly and plaintively.

Jubal saw movement off to the east, barely visible in the thick dusk. It was the faint form of a horse and rider. The Spencer swung, aimed and cracked twice. Red lances of flame lashed out.

The figure vanished into the murk of the night.

CHAPTER 11

Ghost Walker, his face rigid with anger, sped up to Jubal.
"Fool! Fool! You should not have killed the Cheyenne," he
yelled. "You have betrayed my honor by interfering. He
should have been safe from you unless I was slain. Then you
could have made your decision of what to do."

"Ease up," retorted Clason, his own irritation rising at the
Indian's biting words. "I just might have kept you from
getting all shot up. Now we can get on with finding someone
with gold."

For a handful of seconds the Arapaho considered raising
his bow and driving an arrow through Clason. The white man
had no honor, as Old Pony Man had warned him. If he
continued to travel with this man Clason, Ghost Walker could
lose the truth of how a man should act before an enemy.

But then there had been members of his own tribe that
were no better than Clason. Black Hand had lied about Ghost
Walker's death to Bird Flying and her parents so he could
possess her. And then Ghost Walker had lain with Bird
Flying and had slain Black Hand. He had thought the provo-
cation severe enough to do those things. The same as Clason
thought his desire for gold and his need for Ghost Walker to
help him get that gold was sufficient reason to kill the
Cheyenne.

Clason had read the passions chasing across Ghost Walker's
countenance. When the Arapaho's hand had clinched upon
the bow, Jubal had readied his own reflexes for action. He

was not going to calmly sit and let the Indian stick an arrow through him.

"It is done. Do we fight over it now?" Clason asked curtly.

Ghost Walker shook his head disgustedly and his mouth closed like a grim trap. He went to the body hanging to the side of the black horse. With a slice of his knife, he severed the thong that attached the Cheyenne to the horse's mane and laid him on the ground. You were a brave warrior, thought Ghost Walker. However, Clason is correct. It is finished. You are finished in this life.

Ghost Walker stripped the buffalo-hide saddle from the Cheyenne's cayuse and hazed the animal away with a clap on the rump. He had no need for another horse. Let it run wild upon the prairie and live many years.

Taking up the reins of his own mount, Ghost Walker led it to the camp. A mound of twists of coarse grass was piled by the embers of the fire. He tossed a double handful on the smoldering coals and flames flared up.

In the flickering light he searched through the dead man's belongings. There was nothing he wanted until he found the painted buckskin shirt where Cloud Woman had dropped it. The pigment was still damp on the animal figures, and in a few places there were smeared black spots on sections where there should have been no paint.

Ghost Walker marveled at the lifelike paintings. He had not expected the crude Cheyenne to have such mastery of decoration. He would take the shirt as his own.

Spreading the garment before the fire to complete its drying, Ghost Walker began to scrape the errant black paint off with his fingernail.

Jubal rode up and stepped down. Darkness was closing them in. "We might need the teepee, for it feels like rain is coming."

"What did you shoot at over that direction?" asked the Arapaho, pointing.

"I saw somebody on a horse."

"This is a woman's camp. There are a woman's things here. What you saw could have been the Cheyenne's squaw."

"Well, it's too dark to trail whoever it was tonight. Tomorrow we'll find out. What is that roasting over the fire?"

"Smells like buffalo hump, the best of food. The Cheyenne are either dead or gone. Let us feast upon their food."

Clason squatted down and cut a slice from the chunk of meat. He was glad to see Ghost Walker had seemingly put the manner of the Cheyenne's death behind him. That was good, for Clason did not want trouble with the Arapaho.

A cold drizzle began to fall. The men staked out their horses and retreated into the teepee with their gear.

Ghost Walker hung the painted buckskin shirt between two of the poles of the lodge. He lay on his pallet and looked at the dead man's garment, visible in the glow of the fire shining through the open portal of the teepee.

"What did you call to me as I went to fight the Cheyenne?"

"That you should give him a rifle and tell him to go kill white men."

Ghost Walker lay pondering what Clason had said. Much strength could be gained by joining forces with the Cheyenne. Perhaps together they could drive the white men from their lands. Was it possible to subdue old hatreds and fight a greater common enemy and thus maybe survive.

The cold rain killed the flames of the fire. The Cheyenne's shirt dissolved into the darkness. Ghost Walker stared where the garment had been. I am sorry you are dead, Cheyenne. You and I would have made good fighting comrades and won many battles.

Susan released her clutch on the double thickness of blankets she had held tightly about her throughout the watch and stood up. In the gathering brightness of the morning, frost showed thick upon the grass and crackled beneath her boots. Nearby, the horses' breaths plumed out in clouds of white.

"Dan, Phil, wake up. It's light enough to see," Susan called to the two men.

Phil mumbled something unintelligible and began to stretch. Dan crawled out of his covering and started to pull on his boots.

The rain clouds of the previous day had dropped below the distant eastern horizon. The dawn was a silent explosion of orange and red in a thin layer of moisture haze.

Susan gazed in wonderment at the gorgeous display of

colors. A new day was born. Perhaps this journey could be made safely. If they were cautious enough.

Her sight drifted down from the heavens to cast about on the dangerous plain of the earth. With its coating of frost the stiff grass glistened like quicksilver. The slight unevenness of the topography was masked by the sameness of the vegetation. A mound of dirt at the entrance of some animal's burrow showed as a black spot.

Susan ranged her scrutiny to the south. She was surprised to see a horse watching her from a quarter mile or so.

"Dan, look quickly, a wild horse," Susan exclaimed.

Dan hastily swung in the same direction. After a moment's evaluation, he said, "Somebody or something appears to be laying on its back. This may be a trick." His voice became sharp. "Phil! Get your rifle ready."

The young man jumped up immediately with his gun. He peered intently across the distance. "Dan, you are right. There's a man on the back of that horse."

"Whoever it is may have deliberately made himself seen so our attention would be toward him," said Dan. He rotated completely around to examine the terrain on all sides. Nothing out of the ordinary was evident.

"Pack up," he ordered. "Let's get ready to ride and then we'll see what should be done about our visitor."

Speedily, the mounts were saddled and the packhorses loaded. Susan and the men kept a vigilant eye on the distant figure. As they worked, the unknown horse came slowly in their direction.

The top curve of the sun crested the horizon and a bright golden ray of light struck the prairie. The strange horse and the form upon it were strongly illuminated.

"It's a man all right," said Dan. "He's holding around the horse's neck."

"Mount up," directed Dan. "We'll go have a look. Watch on all sides. This still could be a trap."

Watching the humans with wide, alert eyes, the strange cayuse turned sideways and prepared to run away. The buckskin-clad figure it carried was plainly visible.

"I see blood on the man's back," said Susan. "He could be hurt bad or dead."

Dan spoke to the horse in a low, soothing voice. "Easy there, Indian pony. Who are you carrying?"

The cayuse stood its ground and Dan caught the leather reins of its bridle.

"Phil, see what we have here," Dan said. "Susan, keep a lookout."

Phil stepped down and went to the figure. "He's stiff and dead. And it's a woman, not a man. A pretty, young Indian woman."

He unclasped her cold, rigid arms and hands from around the pony's neck. He lifted her down from the buffalo-hide saddle and placed her gently on the ground.

"She's been shot by a rifle or pistol up high in the back. Bullet went clear through her. The blood is dry, so it must have happened some time ago."

"Indians fighting each other, I suppose," said Dan. "Or a white man could have done it."

"She sure did hold onto her pony, even while dead," Phil said in a low, sad voice. He returned to the woman's mount and began to go through the pouches fastened to its back.

"Susan, look at this." Phil held up a brightly painted buckskin shirt for his sister to see.

"Oh, how lovely," exclaimed Susan. "She would be very beautiful wearing that."

She fingered the pliable material. The texture was very pleasant to her skin and the painted designs and landscapes delighted her sight.

Dan noted the pleased expression on his wife's face. "Why don't you take it," he suggested.

"It is a true work of art," said Susan. "Do you think it would be proper for me to keep it? I feel odd about doing it."

"The poor woman is dead," responded Dan. "She has no more use for it. If left out in the open, the sun and rain will shortly destroy it. I believe she would want you to have it. A gift from one pretty woman to another."

Susan regarded the Indian woman lying so still in the grass. "She was beautiful, wasn't she? Yes. I will take the garment. I am sad that her people will never know what happened to her. However, I will remember her each time I wear this shirt and will say a prayer for her."

"We had best be on our way," said Dan, glancing anxiously over the prairie. "Get aboard, Phil, and let's move on."

"Wait," called Susan, annoyance ringing in her tone. "Do we rob the dead and then just ride away and let the coyotes and buzzards eat them. She has given us a valuable gift. We must bury her decently."

"Susan, we should be riding fast toward St. Joe," said Dan. "There may be Indians or white men close who would attack us."

"No. We can spare an hour to place her properly in the ground so the animals and birds do not feed on her. Phil, get a shovel from the packs."

"Dan's right, sis. We should go now," said Phil.

"Both of you listen to me. We do the right thing by her." Susan's voice was adamant. "Or I will stay here and do it myself."

"We will do what you want, sis," responded Phil.

Dan nodded agreement. "Keep lookout, Susan, while I help Phil." He climbed down from his horse.

Susan pulled her rifle from its scabbard and began to scan the prairie.

When the sun came up and burned away the darkness, Jubal and Ghost Walker took up the trail of the rider that had left the Indian camp. They easily followed the sign at a gallop.

"The pony has been walking except for right there at the very first. Won't take long to catch up," said Jubal.

"Do you think you hit her with your bullets?" asked Ghost Walker.

"So you think it is a her? Well, I'm a fair shot and usually hit what I aim at."

The Arapaho did not like the events of the past few hours. It may have been a bad day when he first encountered this white man. However, he had set his course, the arrow had been let fly and now he must wait and see where it fell. Already they had accumulated several rifles and pistols. And a large quantity of the white man's gold that could be traded for hundreds of rifles. His share was more than enough to arm all the men of his village.

The sun climbed a handwidth higher above the rim of the plain. Ghost Walker observed the pony's tracks begin to meander, as if no longer guided by its rider. He spoke to Jubal.

"We will soon come upon the cayuse."

"Yes, I think you are right. We'll slow down and take more care to check ahead."

The Arapaho had been staring to the front. There were objects on the far skyline. "I see horses there." He pointed.

Jubal shaded his eyes with his hand. "Yep. Several horses. Now I wonder what is going on. Let's find some gully deep enough to hide us and go in close."

The men staked all the horses in a swale where they could not be seen by the distant people, then, armed with rifles, began a cautious, concealed stalk.

Soon they were forced to crawl on hands and knees to remain hidden. Farther along they began to worm forward on their stomachs, parting the grass slowly, bending the thin reeds only when they moved under the puffs of the wind.

"This is as close as we dare go or we'll be seen," whispered Clason, eyeing the group of men two hundred yards away. "I wonder what they are digging for."

"Maybe they dig a grave," said Ghost Walker. "Do you think white men would bury an Indian they came upon?"

"A few might. Most wouldn't. These folks have three packhorses heavy-loaded. All the gear looks of good quality. 'Pears to me, here are some prospectors trying to sneak across the country to go East. They look rich enough to have struck gold. Let's take a few shots at them and go have a look at what they carry."

The two men that had been working stopped their labor. One went to a packhorse and put a shovel in a pack. Both moved toward their mounts.

"Kill them before they get to their horses," hissed Clason.

The white man and the Indian rose up from the prairie grass to a kneeling position and began to shoot.

Susan heard the chilling crack of a rifle. She saw Phil grab at his chest and spin around under the impact of the bullet. He fell.

Dan was hit at the same instant. He went down hard. There was a terrible look of pain on his face as he rolled to his

knees and started to crawl toward the rifle in the scabbard on
his horse. He seemed to be having difficulty seeing.

A bullet whizzed past near Susan's cheek. The first fusil-
lade had been aimed at the men. Now the unseen gunmen had
opened up on her. A shot hit the pommel of her saddle and
ricocheted away with a keening whine like some deadly little
animal. She felt the shock in her horse as it was struck in the
head by the next shot.

She kicked her feet free of the stirrups as the horse crashed
to the ground. She landed beside it with a body-battering
slam.

Her addled brain struggled to collect itself. The rifle, she
must find her rifle. Where had it fallen? Dan and Phil needed
her to help fight off the attackers.

The packhorse that had been near Susan reared and squealed
in agony. Fatally wounded, it fell upon Susan and her mount.

The massive body pressed down with an awful might on
the body of the woman. She thought for sure the bones of her
chest were cracking. Her compressed lungs could not expand
to draw in the life sustaining air.

The packhorse, struggling in death throes, slid farther off
the body of the dead horse and settled heavier upon Susan. A
fog of blackness rolled in, dimming the light in her mind.

Time lost its dimension. A distorting film crept across her
eyes. Yet she still felt her pain. Smelled the horse pressed to
the side of her face. The crash of guns became silent.

Two men began to talk in a strange language. Not Spanish
or French, Susan was certain. Was it some Indian dialect?
How long before they discovered she was still alive and
finished what they had started.

One of the men said something about gold, and they both
laughed in high, good spirits.

The sound of the mens' voices faded away. The odor of the
dead horses-dwindled to nothing. The blackness completely
extinguished the light in Susan's mind.

Clason plunged his hand into the leather bag and pulled out
a handful of gold coins. "Look at these, Ghost Walker—real
gold. And in this bag, well, it's crammed with gold dust."

"How much?"

"Hundreds and hundreds of ounces of it. We have done it

again. Who would ever have believed we could hit it lucky twice in a row? I'm rich."

Jubal began to laugh uproariously. He threw himself down on the ground and rolled and laughed and held his sides in glee.

Ghost Walker turned away from the white man and looked at the Indian cayuse and the new grave. Because these people had delayed their travel to bury the Indian woman, they were now dead. The world was an impartial judge and made no more allowances for errors in judgment from those who did humane things than for those who killed and robbed.

When Clason quieted, Ghost Walker spoke to him. "How many rifles will my share of all the gold buy?"

"A thousand maybe, depending on what kind of price you can dicker for. But a thousand warriors with rifles can't beat the Army. You'll need many more guns than that."

"I believe you are correct. I must give each Arapaho and Cheyenne a gun. Then we can make battle with the Army of the white men.

Clason evaluated the young Indian brave. The fellow really thought he could arm his people and whip the U.S. Army. Why, probably only four or five Indians out of a hundred could load a rifle and hit a man at a hundred yards. And where could he buy good rifles of the number he was considering? Jubal himself, a white man, would require months to assemble that many weapons. Ghost Walker was dreaming a mad dream doomed to certain failure.

"We must have much more gold for you to buy that many rifles," Clason said. The Arapaho made a good partner. Let him dream and scheme a little longer.

Ghost Walker said, "Then let us take what we want from these people and search for gold to steal."

CHAPTER 12

The sun shined down from the immense gray-blue sky to warm the broad sweep of prairie. Beside the skin teepee in the shallow swale of the vast plain, the black horse stood guard over the motionless body of the Cheyenne, Fast Running.

As the odor of death from the corpse grew stronger, the faithful beast gradually drew away toward the teepee and the familiar odors that arose there. He could still detect the scent of his master's mate in the hide structure. But that was waning quickly.

Now and then the horse took a bite of grass. As he chewed, he examined the man, wondering why he lay so long upon the ground. Yet no thought of deserting his silent master came to the horse.

Luke moved strongly on the course of the two killers and the five horses they rode and led. The trail was steadily growing colder. The light rain of the night had partially obliterated the hoof prints; however, enough of the faint indentations remained so that taken together with the broken stems of grass, he could follow at a fast walk.

Luke worried that a hard rain, common on the prairie in the autumn, would destroy the sign entirely. That would leave him wandering hopelessly in search of his enemies. For now, though, no indication of foul weather existed. Overhead, the sun sailed high and bright in the sky.

The land fell away at a slight incline. Immediately, Luke spotted the hide teepee and the tall, black horse.

The teepee was small, like the Cheyenne sometimes used for temporary shelter while traveling. Its presence meant a woman was with the party. Men hunting game or on the war trail would consider such a cumbersome contrivance a dangerous impediment to their need for swift passage over the land.

Luke evaluated the camp for a few minutes. The painted designs on the lodge convinced him this was a Cheyenne camp. The tracks he had followed had led him to this very place. What was the relationship between the two groups of people? Was the meeting accidental or prearranged?

No living thing stirred except the horse. The animal's gaze shifted from Coldiron to something on the ground near it.

Guardedly, Luke went forward. The occupants of the lodge might return at any moment. He wanted to capture the black horse and be long gone before that happened.

The mustang snorted and tossed its head. It spun about as if to retreat from the strange man that approached. Then again it looked at its master and stood its ground.

Closer now, Coldiron saw the body in the grass. From the unnatural, crumpled slackness, he knew the man was dead. The outlaws who had attacked Luke had continued their deadly work upon the Cheyenne. Was the woman dead somewhere near, or had the outlaws taken her with them?

Luke slipped his belt from his waist and held it coiled in a hand. He extended his other hand and started to talk low and gentle to the mustang. The horse was an outstanding animal, perhaps the war pony of the Indian. If so, it would be the strongest and most intelligent beast the Cheyenne could obtain.

One of the most important things that a war pony was taught was to stand and wait for its rider to remount after a fall. Now the gold-flecked black eyes of the brute watched Luke intently as it wavered with indecision as to whether to remain near Fast Running or try to escape from this new man drawing very near.

The outstretched fingers touched the velvet-smooth nose of the mustang. It trembled at the contact. Then the man caressed the long, bony jaw. "Well, it seems like you and I might get along together."

Luke encircled the horse's neck with the belt and then, holding tightly to it, rubbed firmly over the broad back with

the palm of a hand. The horse's tail flicked and the muscular
body tightened in anticipation of taking a rider's weight.
Luke noted the animal's action and jumped to lay across its
back. Instantly, he threw a leg over and sat up.

The cayuse pivoted. His rump came up half-heartedly in a
buck. He stopped and turned to smell of Coldiron's leg.

"I expected more from you than that," Luke told the
horse. He petted the glossy neck and spoke soothingly. "Relax, old buddy, I'm sure not going to hurt you."

Coldiron dismounted and led the mustang to the teepee.
No saddle or bridle was found. Casting about in an ever
widening circle, he found the riding gear where Ghost Walker
had discarded it.

"I guess they had all the mounts they needed," Coldiron
said to the horse as he tightened the buffalo-hide saddle upon
its back. Now, instead of trekking thirty miles on foot in a
long day, his range of travel would be lengthened to fifty
miles or better on the back of this good mount.

Luke felt his desire for revenge surge hot within him. From
here on he would gain upon the thieves.

Selecting from the sparse possessions of the Indians, Luke
assembled a pack. Among his finds was a bag of pemmican,
five pounds or so of shredded meat, suet, marrow and all
sweetened with wild cherries. He could live for days on the
pemmican alone. He fastened the pack on the horse, yanked
himself astride, and left at once, hounding the trail of his
foes.

Beneath the great bowl of the pale blue sky, the big black
ran easily, swinging his powerful legs, devouring mile after
mile of the grass-covered prairie. Luke tuned himself to the
rocking lope of the Cheyenne war pony and probed ahead for
the trail.

Poor bastards, thought Coldiron, gazing down at the bodies of the two men sprawled on the earth and a third crushed
beneath a horse with only the lower half of his body showing.
The men he was pursuing had wantonly slain again. It was a
tragedy and he was sorry for the dead.

Luke checked quickly for weapons. Every holster and
scabbard was empty.

Four horses had been cut down by bullets during the battle.

Two others stood off a short ways, watching. Saddles and packs had been removed from the live animals and dumped on the ground. Coldiron caught one of the horses that still showed the sweaty outline of the packs it had carried.

Luke skimmed his view over the provisions strewn about. It appeared only the guns and ammunition had been taken. From this ample supply of goods, he could completely outfit himself except for a rifle.

A weak, pain-filled moan sounded from the figure trapped under the horse. Luke hastily went to kneel beside the man. The method of the outlaws was to leave none of their victims alive. This time they had made a mistake; a man still lived.

"Take it easy, fellow," Luke said. "I'll get this horse off you in a little bit. How bad are you hurt?"

Silence answered him.

Luke appraised the position of the one dead horse lying upon the other. He noted the support provided by the body of the bottom animal. One false move in freeing the man and the full weight of the top horse, a half ton or more, would fall upon him. The top body would have to be rolled off carefully.

The packhorse was led up. Two ropes were looped around its neck to extend backward, one on each side past its flanks and over the dead horse. Luke cut slits between tendon and bone on two of the dead horse's legs, and there inserted the ropes where they could not slip loose.

"Giddap!" Luke commanded the packhorse. The brute leaned strongly into the makeshift harness. Luke heaved mightily on the carcass at the same instant, trying to hold the weight off the pinned man. The dead horse rotated to lay on its spine. The stiff legs pointed skyward for a moment and then the body continued its roll to flop on the ground.

Coldiron squatted, expecting to find a man. Instead, he saw the fine, delicate features of a woman!

She looked dead. Then the chest heaved. A groan came with the exhalation. She breathed hurriedly again, starvingly sucking air. Her hands fluttered like small, half-suffocated animals coming alive.

"You will live," Luke said to the awakening woman. "Can you hear me? You will live."

Her mouth had been mashed against her teeth. Luke wiped caked blood from her lips with a callused finger. The rough texture of the ground was deeply imprinted into her cheek. That mark would disappear and the lips would heal.

Coldiron shifted positions so that his shadow fell to protect her face from the sun. Not knowing how seriously she was hurt, he was afraid to move her. Let her come fully to consciousness and determine her own injuries.

He lowered himself to a seat on the ground. He waited restlessly, inspecting the surrounding terrain. A herd of buffalo was a black splotch on the northern horizon. Nearer to him a falcon hovered fifty feet in the air above a prairie dog town. The graceful bird partially folded its wings and plummeted earthward. It arose with empty talons. Shrieking a lament of failure, it glided off on the breeze.

The sun moved the distance of its diameter across the sky. Coldiron glanced at the woman. Alert brown eyes glared savage hate at him. Her hand was extended to within a finger width of the butt of his six-gun.

He reached out and seized the hand. Immediately, her other hand, the fingers bent like claws, slashed at him. He slapped it aside. "Stop that," he ordered.

Susan jerked back, trying to break free.

"I see you are not much hurt," said Luke. "Now don't strike at me. I am not who you think I am. I just found you and got the dead horse off you."

"Where's my husband? Where's my brother, Phil?"

"There's two dead men here. I guess they are the ones you are asking about."

Susan raised up to look at the slumped bodies of her husband and brother in the grass. She covered her face with her hands and sobbed. The only people who meant anything to her were gone. Her world was destroyed.

Gradually, she gained control of her anguish and swallowed her sobs. She examined the features of the black-haired man above her. An old head wound, swollen and bloody, gave him a wild, animal appearance. Yet the eyes that watched her were friendly.

She believed he spoke the truth. "Then who are you? What are you doing here?"

"My name is Luke Coldiron. I was far over there at the base of the mountains and heading home to my ranch down on the border of the New Mexico Territory. Some bushwhackers killed my horses and left me for dead. They took more than thirty thousand dollars of my gold. I've been on their trail for better than two days now. Luke looked more closely at the woman. "Weren't you in Denver a short time back? Seems like I saw you there."

Susan recognized the cowboy, and the incident in front of the Charpiot Hotel came flooding back. "Yes. My name is Susan Penfold. You threatened me with your pistol."

"Only because of the way you pointed your rifle at me. But that was yesterday. What happened here?"

"Someone hidden in the grass shot at us without warning. It happened so unexpectedly we had no time to defend ourselves. I saw Dan and Phil fall."

"What did the gunmen look like?"

"I never got to see them. After they finished shooting, they came close and I heard them talk in a strange language."

Luke rubbed his whiskered chin. The woman would be no help to him. Time was wasting and he should be riding. "Can you stand up?"

"I think so." She climbed feebly to her feet. "Yes. I am all right. A little shaky, that's all."

"Then let's pack you some supplies," said Luke.

Susan did not hear him. She stumbled close to kneel by the side of Dan's body and then beside Phil. Luke heard her sad cries.

He caught the last horse and saddled it. From time to time as he prepared a pack for the woman, he glanced at her sitting midway between the dead men.

"I must be going now," Coldiron had led up the horse he meant for her to use. "The outlaws who killed your men and took my gold are getting farther and farther ahead of me."

The woman shook herself as if coming awake from a deep sleep. "They stole our gold, too. I'm sure that's why they attacked us."

"I've looked through the packs and did not see any gold. How much did you have?"

"About seven hundred ounces."

"That much, eh. With what the robbers took from you and me, they probably feel rich. Most likely they'll ride straight out of the country."

"Oh! Damn them all to hell!" exploded Susan. "If they were here and I had a gun, I'd kill them, every one."

"I could not find a gun. The outlaws are taking every one they find. Where were your men fighting? I would like to search there. Just maybe a rifle was overlooked."

"From where Dan and Phil are lying, I don't think they ever got their rifles off the horses."

"Where was your gun when your horse fell on you?"

"I don't know. I was mounted and holding the rifle when the bullets hit. I think I threw the gun away from me so I wouldn't fall on it."

"Show me how you might have done it. The grass is deep and maybe the gun wasn't found."

"I was facing the grave like this. When the horse started to go down, I shoved the rifle off in that direction." Susan made a motion with her hands.

"Fine. I'll look around in that spot." He walked about parting the slender stems of the knee-high grass.

"Damnation. What luck. Here it is." Luke dragged the long weapon out from under a clump of matted-down grass.

He shook it happily and then levered open the breech. "A Henry repeating rifle. Works fine as a new one. This sure helps to even the odds."

He emptied the cartridges in a pile on the ground. After wiping them clean on the leg of his pants, he reinserted them into the long tube beneath the barrel. "Only seventeen shells. You could have had one more cartridge in it."

"That seemed enough at the time," replied Susan.

"They'll serve me very well. Now to run the outlaws down. As fast as they were traveling, that will take many long days of riding and some good luck. I must get on their trail before it gets older. Before I leave, I'll help you bury your dead."

"I am to blame for their deaths."

"How is that possible?"

"They did not want to bury the Indian woman. I insisted they do it, and in the time that took, the bandits found us and killed them."

Luke had seen the fresh grave. That explained the Cheyenne's missing squaw. "You could not know the outlaws would be trailing the woman."

"A person must always expect the worst to happen and prepare for it."

"That is surely true. Too bad you had to pay such a high price to learn it. Is it okay if I bury them by the Cheyenne woman?"

"Yes. That would be fine. If there is a spirit world, she should be good company for them."

Coldiron worked swiftly. The dark, rich prairie soil came up damp and soft on the blade of the shovel. Soon a double-width grave stood open and waiting.

Together Susan and Luke wrapped the men in their sleeping blankets and tied the covering fast with short lengths of rope.

Luke stepped down into the excavation and, reaching out, pulled the bodies to him and gently placed them in the bottom.

"Before you climb out, would you please straighten and smooth the blankets, Mr. Coldiron?"

Luke noticed the taut muscles in the woman's jawline and her hands entangled and gripping each other. She was on the verge of breaking. "Certainly," he replied, and tucked the wool cloth in neatly around the still forms.

Luke hoisted himself out and stood by the woman. "Do you want to say a prayer?"

"No. I want to make a vow." She faced the open grave squarely and stared at the corpses. "Dan, Phil, hear me. You have been slain and will never be with me again. Oh, how much I miss you. But rest easy, for I make this solemn oath that I will find whoever did this terrible thing and kill them. Kill them without mercy or warning as they did you."

Her voice rose to a shrill, piercing shriek, wavering and undulating from one high note to another. Luke's heart thudded wildly in response to the intensity of the suffering in the cry. Then in the space of one note, her scream of sorrow altered to a fierce, savage shriek full of the threat of vengeance.

Susan's voice sank to a rasping hiss. "Be prepared, my loved ones, for I will send the bastards to you soon."

"That's no way to end a funeral," Luke admonished Susan.

She paid him no heed, as if not hearing. She took the shovel from his hands and began to fill the grave. As she fought the dirt, she said over and over in a guttural tone, "I promise! I promise!"

The prairie soil fell heavy upon the bodies.

Coldiron walked away from the woman as she toiled with the shovel. He selected articles from the assortment of supplies the outlaws had scattered on the ground in their search for valuables. A full complement of gear and food was soon assembled. A bundle of clothing containing pants, shirt and wool coat that appeared to be about the correct size to fit him was found. It would be very useful if he should get caught in a rainstorm. He tossed it on the pile of provisions. An extra blanket topped it off.

Luke loaded all the paraphernalia on the packhorse and covered everything with a large piece of canvas. The waterproof covering would serve as a tight shelter.

The crude buffalo-hide saddle on the black horse was replaced with one of the white men's saddles. It was time to depart, and he felt relief at the thought of getting away from the bereaved woman. He led the woman's horse to her.

"Denver is straight west," Luke told the woman. "You should be able to reach it in two days or a little longer. I'm sorry I don't have a gun to give you, but I'll need both the rifle and pistol. With luck, you'll reach town without any trouble."

"Did the killers go toward Denver?" asked Susan, her attention focusing on Luke.

"No, they went off to the east."

"Then that's the way I will go."

"Look, I know you made an oath to catch them, but I'll do that. You go to Denver where it's safe."

"Don't talk to me like I'm a child," snapped Susan, her resentful eyes burning at him. "I have a riding horse and a packhorse. And a rifle if you'll give it back to me. I'm going after those sons of bitches. That is my horse you have that pack on, isn't it?"

"Yes. But I intend to use it."

"It is mine and I will take it with me. Give me my rifle." Her voice shook with a controlled fury. "You are the one that does not have the right equipment."

"I should have left you under that dead horse to die," growled Coldiron, furious at the contrariness of the woman.

"I did not ask you for help," snapped Susan.

"That's correct. However, I did help you and for that my charge is one packhorse and all he can carry. And one rifle." Luke threw down the reins of her riding horse and, grabbing up the lead line of the pack animal, stepped astride the black horse. Without a backward glance, he left at a gallop.

Susan turned slowly, seeing the bodies of the four dead horses, the fresh dirt of the graves and the blood on the broken and flattened grass where Dan and Phil had died. She sobbed in spite of herself.

Hurriedly, she found a hat, a heavy coat, a rain slicker, and gathered a few other necessary items for a journey whose length she could not even begin to guess. A journey that would end in her death or the death of the men she would take revenge on.

She rolled her small collection of possessions into a pair of blankets and fastened the bundle behind the saddle. Pulling herself astride, she kicked her mount into a run after the rider on the black horse, fast drawing distant on the plain.

She felt deserted and lonely. All she owned in the world was a horse, a saddle, and a tiny parcel of clothing. No, that was not all; she owned a covenant with two dead men and enough hate to carry it through.

CHAPTER 13

The afternoon waned, the sun sank and it was night. Coldiron hounded the trail until the last bit of daylight had leaked away into the sky. He halted where the darkness overtook him. His enemies had outdistanced him and were farther ahead than when the day had begun.

He knew the woman followed; however, he gave no sign to her. She was a nuisance and would be a dangerous hindrance when the fight commenced. Short of beating her, he knew of no way to turn her back.

As he staked out the horses, she rode in. She sat watching him, her body slumped wearily in the saddle. She saw the stiffness in his movements and the way he favored his back. For the first time she realized he must have a second wound.

Luke spread his buffalo-hide bed and dug out provisions for a cold supper. The woman climbed down and tethered her horse so it could graze. Without a word to Coldiron she tossed her bodroll on the ground and came to kneel beside the pack of supplies he had brought. Sorting through the various items mostly by touch, she separated out food for herself. Scooping up what she had found, she walked off into the darkness.

Silently she ate, a hunched dark form on the prairie grass.

Coldiron lay down on the sleeping robe and tugged it over himself. His pistol lay touching his fingers. He took three breaths and was fast asleep.

Sometime later Luke came awake in one fractional tick of

time and his hand closed on the butt of his six-gun. The echo of a heartrending sob lay on the night. He listened for the woman to cry out again.

He did not know where she had finally lain down and gone to sleep. That was not good. Whether he liked her presence or not, closer attention must be paid to her.

The woman made no further sound. Yet he sensed her wakefulness out there somewhere in the darkness. She had received a grievous blow. But only she could resolve to accept her loss and conquer her sorrow. Luke still felt his own poignant sadness at the death of his old friend Yerrington. The woman's grief must be far more soul-bending than even that.

Luke checked the position of the stars and judged the night still young. He rested. Above him the moon slid across the heavens. The wind sighed and the horses made low tearing sounds as they cropped the prairie grass. A peacefulness seemed to pervade the night-shrouded prairie. Coldiron knew it as a false peace. Scores of violent men prowled the plains and the mountains. Two of them he would find and kill.

In the uncertain light of first dawn, Coldiron threw aside his frost-cloaked robe, pulled on his boots and stood up.

Fifty yards away the woman was kneeling on the ground and looking to the east. For a moment Luke wondered what she was doing. Then he realized she was exactly on the trail of the outlaws and facing in the direction they had gone.

The frost has hidden the sign, she called over her shoulder without glancing at Luke.

"Once it melts, the sign will be visible again and we will be able to follow easily. Even now I can track them."

"Well, if you can, then let's be about it," she replied curtly.

She went hastily to her blankets and began to roll them up. As she passed, Luke saw her face, taut and twisted. Her total being, bent upon revenge, had made her an ugly woman.

The sun burned the white frost and sucked up the moisture. The miles slid past beneath the hurrying feet of the horses. Luke stopped at noon.

"What's the matter? Are you too tender to ride all day?" Susan asked brusquely.

"I don't stop because of me," Luke responded testily. "The ponies need a rest." Then his anger ebbed as he saw the haunted expression in her eyes.

Luke reclined on the ground near the horses. Susan paced back and forth a short distance along the course while she waited.

"Better rest while you have a chance," Luke called to her.

Susan did not bother to answer.

The chase was taken up again. For the remainder of the day the course headed unswervingly to the east. Luke believed the men had decided they had stolen sufficient gold to satisfy their greed and now were heading for St. Joe.

The darkness came. A silent camp was made in the edge of night.

The frost of the new morning was heavier than the day before. The wind was slow, cold and damp. Luke knew the weather was preparing to change.

The footfalls of the horses measured off the long hours of travel. Though they rode steadily, they gained but little on the bandits. By late afternoon thin, high clouds, like the wide tail of white swans were flying in from the west.

Near dark they came to a small stream and stopped. Coldiron staked out the horses. For the first time Susan prepared an evening meal for both herself and Luke. She did not speak, nor did Luke attempt conversation.

In the middle of the night, Luke heard the sound of a buffalo herd moving slowly in around their camp. He raised up once to evaluate the black forms of the large, humpbacked animals ghosting close in the dark. The horses snorted and stamped the ground complainingly, for they did not like the smell of the shaggy beast.

Luke called out softly to Susan. "The buffalo will not harm you. It is safer with them here, for no one would think to look among them for us."

Some of the inquisitive buffalo drifted near the bedded humans and the packs. One animal emptied himself, the droppings falling with wet plops on the earth. Luke hoped none got on the saddles or provisions. He went to sleep with the musky animal odor strong in his nostrils.

*   *   *

Luke shoved aside his sleeping robe and sat up. A dense overcast hung low and dripped nearly invisible moisture upon the ground and grass. Patches of ground fog hid sections of the prairie. Buffalo drifted through the fog like specters.

A young bull buffalo was at the packs mouthing and licking the wooden handle of the shovel. Susan was awake and curiously observing the animal.

"Friendly brute," she said. "They are almost as friendly as cattle."

So she has finally decided to talk to me, thought Luke. He noted that the stricken cast to her eyes of the days before had somewhat disappeared and the lines in her face had smoothed. Some of her prettiness was returning, even though her full lips were still turned down in a sorrowful curve.

He motioned at the hundreds of buffalo grazing or lying on the plain. "They are unpredictable. I've seen a bunch of them stand and let a man shoot dozens of them and they would not move. Other times they will stampede at the cry of a crow. That one there trying to eat the shovel handle likes the salt that's soaked into the wood from our sweaty hands."

The young bull switched his short tail and twisted about to gaze at the two humans. His black, bulbous eyes examined them minutely. Then nonchalantly, he ambled off.

Luke went to retrieve the horses. They had grown accustomed to the visiting buffalo and were grazing contentedly. By the time Luke had saddled and packed the horses, the buffalo, though seemingly not bothered by Susan and Luke, had drawn away more than a quarter mile.

Susan and Luke rode through the ring of buffalo, the animals retreating to give them a wide berth. Luke found the outlaw's sign beyond the area disturbed by the herd. The west wind shoved the two riders along the trail and the miles slipped away behind them.

"There are two men far off there on the right," said Luke, pointing. "I see no horses. Keep alert."

"Do you think they are the ones we're after?" asked Susan.

"It's the right number all right. But these men are south of the trail we've been on. And where are their horses? Our men had five of them."

The men seemed to see Luke and Susan for the first time. One waved widely overhead, beckoning to them.

"Let's not stop," Susan said.

"Got to. Can't simply pass them by with them asking for help. One is carrying a heavy load on his back. Mighty strange-looking pack."

"This will slow us down. Please, let's go on and not waste time on them," implored Susan.

"Can't rightly do that," Luke brushed aside the tail of his coat so his draw of the six-gun would not be impeded. "We don't know what they might want or do. Stay on my left where I can see you. If trouble starts, ride fast back the way we came."

They came warily through the tall grass to the men. The one with the load was very young. He laid his burden, the unconcious form of an old man, tenderly down on the earth.

The second man, of middle age, handed one of the two repeating rifles he carried to the youth. Both men had rusty-colored hair and ruddy complexions. Their facial features were similar. Luke judged them father and son.

"Howdy," the older man greeted Susan and Luke.

"Hello, yourself," answered Luke.

"Right pleased to see men and riding horses," said the man. His eyes ranged over Susan and Coldiron and along the sides of their horses where rifle scabbards would be fastened. He saw only one rifle, on the man's horse.

He peered at Susan. "Howdy do, ma'am." He lifted his hat and then replaced it on his head. "Take off your hat to the pretty woman, Denzele."

"Sure, Pa." The young man glanced self-consciously at Susan and doffed his hat. "Pleased to see you, ma'am," he said.

"It's good to teach young men manners, don't you think?" said the father to Coldiron. "They should always show respect to womankind." He half closed one eye and measured the black-haired man with the wound on his head.

Coldiron sat silently and waited. There was more to this than a chance encounter on the prairie.

The man on the ground coughed raggedly. He was ancient, worn and bent by weather and time. His face was crowded with a web of wrinkles. He was toothless and his jaws seemed collapsible. Luke was surprised that a man so old still lived.

He coughed again. Blood oozed between his paper-thin lips.

"Grandpa's bleeding at the mouth some more," said Denzele. He started to move to the figure of his relative.

"Denzele! Stay where you are," the father commanded sharply.

The young man stepped back and gripped his rifle.

"We've come from Kentucky to dig gold in the mountains of Colorado," the father said. "Doing right fine until Indians hit us three days ago. They run off our horses and drove an arrow through my dad here. 'Pears the point nicked his lungs, for he's been coughing up blood. We've been toting him on our backs for better than a half hundred miles. We want to get him to Denver City and a doctor so he won't die. That needs to be done faster than we can carry him. We got only a little money, but we want to buy one of your horses for him to ride."

"You can see that we have only one packhorse," Susan said to the man. "We need it, for we've got a long journey ahead."

Luke looked into the stern face of the woman. "They need the horse worse than we do."

Susan spoke, short and blunt. "None of our horses are for sale."

"Ma'am, saving a man's life is 'bout as important a thing as a person can do. We want a horse. The pack one will do."

"No!" exclaimed Susan. "The horses stay with us."

"You're a stubborn woman," said the man. "We want only one animal. Then you can go on your way. We are honest men. But you must understand that old man there is blood relation. Do you know what that means back where we come from?"

"You can't have it," Susan said harshly.

"What do you say, mister?" asked the man. His stance shifted ever so slightly. Denzele tensed.

"I guess the answer is no, for the horses belong to her."

Luke saw the man's breathing become shallow and a hardness come into his eyes. Gunplay was now. Coldiron spoke warningly to the Kentucky men. "I can draw my six-gun and shoot both of you faster than you can swing those rifles on me. Don't force me to kill you."

"I've heard tell some of you fellows are mighty quick with handguns. But we've had considerable practice with these here rifles."

"I believe you would trade your life for your dad's. But what is your son's life worth?"

The Kentucky man blinked once. The man on the horse was not one to bluff. "We will pay all the money we got for one horse. That's nearly a hundred dollars."

"The woman says no sale," responded Coldiron.

"I was hoping it wouldn't come to this. But still I thought it might. So we're going to take it. Look over there on your right and behind. My two older sons are there with a dead bead on you."

"Susan, take a look," directed Coldiron, his sight never leaving the two men before him.

"They are there, just like he says." Susan's voice trembled.

Luke turned. Two tall young men aimed rifles at him. Some broken grass, part of that which had camouflaged them, still clung to their clothing. The trap had been prepared before he and Susan had ridden close.

"I have told them to kill if we could not buy a horse. They will do exactly that. We mean you no harm except to take one horse. Put your hands over your heads."

Luke did as ordered. The father came swiftly and plucked the pistol from Luke's holster. "I don't want you to hurt one of my boys or us to hurt you. You may take what you want from the packs and tie it behind you."

"You said you were honest men, and yet you steal," Susan said in a scalding voice.

"To be an honest man is very important to me," replied the father. "Only one thing would make me turn away from that. And that is the life of one of my family. To keep them safe, I would fight Satan himself." He spoke to Luke. "Pick what you want, for we both are in a hurry."

"Help me," Luke said to Susan. He stepped down and went to the packhorse. She followed and they collected several items, wrapped some in the canvas and some inside blankets, and tied the bulky rolls behind the saddles. Susan returned to the packs and pulled out the Cheyenne woman's buckskin shirt and jerked it on.

"Here is your pistol," said the father. "And the cartridges for it. Don't try to reload until you are out of rifle range."

He turned and studied Susan for a moment. Then dug in a pocket and brought out a small leather pouch. "There is ninety-three dollars in gold and paper money in this. It is all yours for the horse."

"I want no money from you," retorted Susan.

The man moved his shoulders in a slight shrug. "I'm truly sorry about this happening." He slipped the money back into his pocket. "Denzele, you weigh the least. Climb up on the horse so you can hold your grandpa on."

"Sure, Pa." The youngest of the clan tossed his rifle to a brother and vaulted up on the back of the animal. Carefully, the pale old man was lifted up from the ground and set astride in front. Denzele cradled the slack body between his arms, gripped the reins of the crude halter and kicked the horse into motion.

"I hope you make it in time to save his life," Luke told the Kentucky man.

"Thanks," the father replied. "My name is Lafe Pertusset. What is your name, so that one day I might return this horse or a better one?"

"Luke Coldiron. But like I said, the horse does not belong to me.

The man questioned Susan. "What is your name, and where can I find you?"

"I want nothing from you," Susan said bitterly, and roughly reined her mount and rode off.

"We are looking for two men with five horses," Luke said to the Kentucky men. "They robbed me and later the party the woman was with. Killed her husband and brother. They should be about a day ahead of us. Have you seen them?"

"Nope. You and the woman are the first humans to cross our path in half a dozen days." The man had been staring after Susan. He turned and squinted at Coldiron. "So that's what is eating at her. Still she's a damn contrary woman. I'm not sure I'd want to travel with her."

"The choice wasn't mine," said Coldiron. He touched the

black horse with his heel and galloped to catch up with Susan.

"They stole our horse," Susan said heatedly.

"Your horse," corrected Luke.

"You think I was wrong. You wanted to give it to them."

"They needed it more than we did."

"We could bring only half of what we had in the packs."

"It is enough. We can make do."

"To hell with you," cried Susan. "I will not let anyone or anything slow me down if I can help it. Do you hear me? Nothing." Yet inside, she was not entirely confident she was right.

"You truly are a contrary woman," said Coldiron. "Now stop arguing with me."

Susan opened her mouth to lash out again at Luke. She caught his eyes glinting at her with a hot anger. He had been pushed to the limit of his tolerance. She had verbally attacked him after he had taken her side against the men from Kentucky, gambling his own life to kill them if they should try to take her horse. Even when he thought her wrong.

She clamped her mouth shut. What a fool she was. He could be a violent man if pressed. She would not blame him if he reached and struck her from her horse, or rode off and left her on the prairie alone.

Luke was glad the woman had finally shut up. Best stay away from her, for she was unpleasant company.

He turned away from Susan and galloped forward along the trail. His eyes leaped the miles ahead, scanning the plain lying beneath the heavy overcast.

In midafteroon the trail of the killers veered to the northeast. Then an hour later to the southeast. At the third turn, one back to the northeast, Coldiron halted and sat his mount.

"Why are they turning first one way and then another?" asked Susan.

"I thought for a while that they were heading straight for St. Joe. Now I believe they are looking for more people to rob. The road between Denver and St. Joe is not just one narrow way. There is a main wagon road that most of the people follow, but there are also several other paths running parallel over a width of five miles or so. The men are swerving back and forth to cover all the trails."

"I wish they had found those Kentucky men," said Susan.

"That would have been a fight worth seeing," said Luke.

"What do we do now?"

"Hang tight to their trail. Once we have sighted them, we will try to get ahead and be lying in wait for them at some good ambush point. Then we'll do to them what they did to you and me," Luke grinned crookedly at Susan. "It'll be very long odds against catching them in just the right spot for us to have the first shots. You should turn back now."

"I'll never stop until they're dead."

"Have it your way. However, it may be you and me that ends up dead."

Following the trail of the outlaws, Susan and Luke changed direction twice more before it became dark. In the gloom of the night the horses slowed and stopped. Luke climbed down and began to untie the bundle of supplies from behind his saddle.

Susan swung down and stood leaning against the side of her horse. "I was wrong about not giving those men a horse. I should have listened to you. They had the greatest need of our extra horse."

"More than your need for revenge?"

"I'll still have that." She began to tug at the leather bindings holding the provisions and her blankets. "I'll have my revenge." Her voice faded, and then came back brittle with her hate. "What those bastards did was so horrible. Dan and Phil were good men."

A few small raindrops struck Luke's face. He smelled the slow, damp wind. "There'll be a hard rain falling in a minute and it's going to be a cold one. With no fire we've got to stay dry or it'll be a miserable night."

Speedily, he staked out the horses, then began to pace about on the ground.

"What are you doing?" questioned Susan, straining to see his vague, dark outline moving erratically about.

"Trying to find a little high piece of ground to make our camp on so the water will run away from us on all sides. Here, I think this spot will do. Quick now, pile all the supplies and saddles here. And our bedrolls, one on each side."

It required only a minute to do as he directed. Luke

unfolded the wide tarpaulin and spread it over the mound of their possessions. The covering extended five feet or so beyond the goods to shelter their beds.

The raindrops became a stream pouring out of the charcoal sky. Luke and Susan scrambled into the space under the canvas. Grateful for the dryness, they unrolled their beds and stretched out.

The night rain swept upon them. It ran soft as the feet of mice across the canvas.

Gradually the intensity of the storm increased. The raindrops grew larger. Soon they were pounding an insane din on the wax-covered canvas.

Luke felt a sense of well-being in the snug haven, the cold wetness held at bay a mere fraction of an inch away. Let tomorrow and the pursuit of the outlaws wait. He relaxed and rested.

"Luke, can you hear me?" called Susan.

"Yes."

"I am sorry for the way I have acted and what I said. Can you forgive me?"

"Sure. It's all right."

She had compassion after all. Perhaps she could be a good comrade on this trail.

"Men shake each other's hand when they have understandings. Will you shake hands with me?"

Luke reached out over the saddles and found her cold fingers. Within his clasp her hand trembled like a small, frightened animal. Instead of releasing her hand, he continued to hold it. As his palm warmed her, he felt the trembling subside.

She was not so tough. Only raw nerve kept her going. He felt sad for her.

As the rain drummed its mad song near Coldiron's ear, a strange thought came to him. The presence of the woman was pleasant. The long night would not be so bad.

CHAPTER 14

Coldiron woke and reached to throw aside the canvas. It was stiff and heavy and did not move under the pressure from his hands. He shoved harder and something came loose from the outside of the canvas and slid with a clatter to the ground.

"Freezing rain must have fallen during the night and we're all iced in," Luke called to Susan.

"You mean we are trapped under here?" Susan's voice had a tinge of alarm.

Luke raised his feet and kicked powerfully upward. The canvas bulged outward and a cascade of broken ice rattled noisily down. He thrust strongly a second time, and a section of the edge of the canvas tore free from where it was imbedded in a sheet of ice on the ground.

"It's going to be okay," Luke assured Susan. He finished ripping loose the covering on his side and, standing up, continued tearing it from the locking hold of the ice on all borders.

Susan stood erect beside Luke. "Oh! How beautiful the colors are," she exclaimed.

All around them as far as the eye could see stretched an ice imprisoned prairie locked in rigid repose. More than a quarter inch of frozen rain encased every object. The grass, its stems weighted and bent with thick rings of ice, dropped in graceful curves like blossoms of crystal flowers. Every blade was visible through the transparent ice sheeting, as if the air itself had condensed and solidified to form the covering.

The first rays of the morning sun slanted in from the eastern horizon and reflected from the flat surface of the ice-clad land with a brilliant silver light. In a thousand places the sunlight entered frozen crystals of pure water, and there within, as though the crystals were the most perfect diamonds, the white light was separated into its component colors and beamed outward to delight the eyes of the man and woman with a shower of gleaming blues, greens and yellows, and all the other colors of the rainbow.

Luke and Susan stood in silent wonder of the kaleidoscope of sparkling radiance. As the sun rose, one diamond point of light after another winked out, only to be replaced by an equally beautiful one at another point.

"Luke, look. There is something fastened inside that clump of grass over there." Susan pointed. "It's a bird, poor thing."

"Yes. I see it. Must have gone in under there to find some protection from the storm. Then got trapped as the grass bent down and froze. Let me get it free."

Walking gingerly on the slick ice, Luke made his way to the small, cold prison. He broke the bars made of ice and stems of grass and caught the gray bird in his hands.

"It's a quail," he said as he held the black-eyed bird aloft for Susan to see. "Strange it should be by itself. Usually, several quail covey together and huddle in a tight knot for warmth during the night."

"It is very pretty," said Susan.

"Then you want me to turn it loose instead of us eating it?" responded Luke. He grinned and looked closely at the woman.

"Oh yes. I do not want to kill it. Let it go. I want to see it fly." There was a hint of a smile in the back of her eyes at his teasing.

Still watching the woman, Coldiron tossed the quail gently into the moring air. As the feathered aviator strongly stroked the breeze and darted away over the bejeweled landscape, Susan's hidden smile escaped to part her full lips. She laughed lightly with pleasure. For the very first time Luke saw her face as it was truly meant to be. And she was beautiful.

Susan glanced at Luke and his grin broadened to match her smile. Then the moment was past and her countenance sobered.

Coldiron saw the change and he accepted it. He spoke.

"It'll take an hour or so for the ice to melt so the horses can stay on their feet and travel. Let's eat and pack while we wait."

"After that heavy rain last night, we've surely lost the trail," said Susan.

"Only for a few hours. It's out there less than a day's ride east. The tracks will be fresh and deep in the wet ground. I'll know them easy for one horse has its right front shoe broken and a second has exceptionally small hooves. We'll hold a course a little south of east until noon and then a little north of east for the remainder of the day. I'm betting we will cross their sign before dark.

Luke and Susan rode into a blustery north wind that flopped the wide brims of their hats and whipped the long tails of the horses. Susan said not a word, as if the one moment of expressed pleasure when the bird had been released had drained her of all desire to talk.

In midafteroon Luke spotted the tracks of five horses in the grass and mud. He dismounted and squatted to intently evaluate them. After a moment he straightened up and swept his gaze to the west along the path. "It's the same horses we have been trailing all these days," Luke said.

"But they are heading in the opposite direction from when we last saw them," said Susan.

"That's strange all right," answered Luke. In the far distance on the other side of many miles of prairie, the Rocky Mountains were shrunk to a range of hills on the horizon. Denver lay there. That was the only town for hundreds of miles in any direction.

"I'd say the outlaws have given up finding somebody to rob out here on the plains. They're probably returning to Denver. We must have passed within a couple of miles of them. By the age of the sign, not more than three or four hours ago."

"We will catch them soon now," said Susan. Her heart sped its beat at the thought.

"Are you still sure you want to find them?" asked Luke.

"Yes. Those killers must not be allowed to live."

"Let's be certain they are the ones to die and not us," replied Luke. He reached for the reins of his horse.

*   *   *

"The men no longer exist. Ghost horses are making these tracks for us to follow," said Susan.

"It might seem so," answered Luke. Four long days of riding through strong winds and on-again off-again rain had passed since the outlaws had reversed direction. He and Susan were often wet, and always cold. She had grown gaunt and her eyes were set in deep hollows. They shined with a strange luminousness, as if she had a fever. Though she had never complained once, Luke was worried about her.

He looked along the muddy trail of the horses that had gone before them. The course had been west, passing some twenty miles north of Denver. It had led up off the broad prairie and now was in the valley of the Niwot River where it cut through the pine-cloaked foothills of the Rocky Mountains.

The storm that had dropped rain on the plains had thrown down deep snow on the tall Rockies. The sharp demarcation between the wet, dark forest of the lower slopes and the snow line was barely a thousand feet above them, yet five miles or so ahead. Another two thousand feet higher, a dense overcast truncated the mountains, hiding the soaring ramparts and turning the massive rock upthrusts into tablelands.

The wind was absolutely still in the valley, and after the blustery noise of the plains an unreal quietness lay upon the land. Mist, like pale smoke, floated down the flanks of the hills and side drainages of the Niwot to coalesce in gray patches of ground clouds in the river bottom.

The quarter-mile-wide valley was dotted with scores of clusters of big ponderosas. Here and there a body of fog had settled around a clump of pines. The high crowns of the trees were black islands reaching above the gray mist.

Luke spoke to Susan. "The outlaws are pushing on as fast as we are. Up higher the deep snow will stop them and they won't be able to climb out of the valley because of the steep walls. Tomorrow we will catch them." Because of the woman Luke was not pleased by the prospect of encountering the killers.

"We can ride late into the evening and make more certain we overhaul them," responded Susan. She was afraid of tomorrow and the battle it might bring. However, she must not show cowardice before this man. For some reason that was important to her.

At snow line Ghost Walker stood on a rocky projection of the mountain and watched his back trail. A great noise drummed in his ears. Close on his right and two hundred feet below, the Niwot River was squeezed in between granite shoulders of the mountain. The flow of the river was a tumbling white cataract, plunging down a steep boulder-choked canyon. The boom and crash of the falling water was flung up out of the chasm to echo off along the slopes and die in the forest.

To the east, the flat bottom of the Niwot River lay spread before him. Groves of pine and many lakes of fog hid most of the bottom. His eyes traced the exact route he and Clason had taken to cross the valley. He saw not one moving thing.

Ghost Walker called out above the noise of the river to Clason. "Somebody follows us. I have felt it for several days. Before we enter the land of snow where every track can be easily seen, I will go back and find out who it is."

Jubal sat his horse on the trail below Ghost Walker. He shifted in the saddle to look up at the Arapaho. "I have thought the same thing. Never once have I seen them. Who could it be?"

Ghost Walker did not answer, and Jubal swung a glance along the river channel and the trail leading up the grade toward him. "I will wait here and keep lookout. Do not go back the way we came. Hold off on the north side of the valley and come in behind them. If they get past you, then I'll stop them here."

Ghost Walker nodded agreement and climbed down the slope to his horse. He dragged his rifle from its scabbard and moved off on foot along a small trail traversing a jutting cleft of rock hanging precariously against the mountainside.

As Luke and Susan crossed the valley, the overcast lowered and a wind began to drone through the rocks and trees. The fog shredded and drifted to the south. Above the thick blanket of clouds, the sun was finishing its slow walk down the ancient sky path. In the hidden valley of the Niwot the gray evening gloom began to gather.

Luke halted and cast his view ahead. The valley was

becoming narrow and the pine forest had thickened. Two miles farther up the drainage, the flanks of the mountain shoved in close to the river and the grade steepened. The snow line commenced there.

Susan examined the canyon of the Niwot and the cold white land lying above her. She questioned Luke. "The river looks like its going to be difficult to travel. How long is it?"

Luke pointed up at the high backbone of the mountain. "It is a short, fast stream. Begins up there near the Continental Divide and flows in a steep grade to the east." He swung his arm to the plains. "Out there beyond the mountains twenty miles or so, it merges with the big South Platte River."

"Why would the men go up into that snowy country with winter coming on?"

"Two years ago gold was found up there another ten miles or so. There's a small settlement called Gold Hill. It should be closing about now, for the snow gets awfully deep. The miners should be coming down from the diggings to Denver for the winter. The outlaws probably plan to rob them. Some of the miners will have their entire summer washing of gold with them.

Coldiron faced the woman. "The outlaws may know we are after them. There's a hundred places where an ambush could be pulled on us. Especially there ahead where the channel is choked in and there's all those trees and boulders. That'd be the best of hiding places. It'll soon be dark. We'd better stop. I'll scout ahead and see if I can find their camp."

"I don't want to be left behind," countered Susan.

"You need to rest, and I'll be back before it gets completely dark. Let's find a place to pitch camp."

He veered from the trail to the right and rode toward the side of the valley where an outcrop of layered rock was visible. As they wound through the large ponderosa pines, icy sleet began to fall in long diagonals from the bellies of the clouds. An ominous hissing sound came to life and filled the woods as the millions of sleet particles struck the needles and boughs of the trees and, glancing downward, bounced and rolled upon the ground.

"I hope we can find a cave or some kind of shelter," said Luke. "We sure do need a dry place to sleep tonight."

Susan silently agreed. She wanted to wrap herself up in

blankets and sleep and sleep. In her weariness her vow of vengeance seemed to be an impossible task.

"There's no cave under the ledges," said Coldiron resignedly. "I'll help you start a lean-to before I leave." He dismounted.

Susan climbed down near Luke. He looked at her through the falling sleet. Some of the white pellets were sticking on the painted Indian shirt. More of them were piling up on the crown and brim of her hat.

Her shoulders were slumped with fatigue and there was a dejected cast to her expression. Luke felt sorrow for her. An overwhelming compulsion to touch her seized him.

He reached out and his fingers brushed the cool softness of her tanned cheek. He wondered what it would be like to spend eternity with this woman.

Her dark eyes shifted to his, suddenly questioning. She stepped back from him. "Why did you do that?"

"It seemed to be the right thing to do and I wanted to," replied Luke.

"My husband has been dead hardly a week. It is not proper for that kind of thing."

A pleasant warmth tingled Luke's nerves. She had not cursed or threatened him. Merely informed him of the recent death of her husband.

"Feelings are important, not time or custom," Luke said.

"They are important to me."

"We are not in Massachusetts where there is a luxury of living according to the codes of a more civilized country. We are in the Colorado Territory and searching for two men to kill. Does that sound like Massachusetts? There the law would be doing the looking, and if the outlaws were caught, a trial would be held. Here, if we catch them, we will kill them. Or they will kill us."

A strong gust of wind swept in and the sleet drummed upon their clothing. A giant pine creaked nearby under the strain of the wind.

Luke continued speaking. "We cannot live here by the customs of back East. We could not survive." He peered intently at her. "Tomorrow we could both be dead."

Her hand moved partway toward him. "Please wait and

ask me again." There was a wistful, contemplative expression to her countenance. "I need time to think."

"That is a fair request. But it will be hard."

A slight smile brightened Susan's face. Then she became solemn and looked away. "It's going to be a bad storm."

Luke allowed her to change the subject. "We'll use the canvas to roof the lean-to." He untied it from behind his saddle and tossed it on the ground.

"It will soon be dark," Susan said. "You go on and see what you can find out about the outlaws. I can build the shelter."

"All right." Luke pulled himself astride the black horse and went off into the forest.

Susan watched Luke disappear into the falling sleet. She looked about for a likely spot to construct the shelter. Two trees eight or nine feet apart were needed so a rope could be stretched between them. Over that support the canvas would be placed and braced to create a protected area beneath.

Leaving her mount tied, she hastened along the rock ledge. All around her the pines bucked and bent as the storm's strength intensified. The course of the wind, interrupted by the forest and the unevenness of the terrain, darted in erratic patterns, driving sleet in under her hat to cut at her face. A tree limb broke and fell crashing to the earth somewhere on her left.

She hurried faster through the thrashing trees and stinging ice pellets. It was a pleasing thought to know there was another friendly human out there somewhere who would return soon.

Susan rounded a large boulder that had rolled down from above. She halted abruptly and her breath caught.

A huge gray wolf crouched beneath a ledge of rock halfway up the face of the bank. It lay with its forepaws drawn up under its chin, and there was a sense of deadly stillness about it that was chilling. Its dark eyes were locked on the human that had invaded its domain.

The wolf came partially erect. It curled back its lips, showing its long teeth, and it growled menacingly.

Susan took a short, halting step backward. The wolf growled again. One ear flicked. The savage eyes flashed beyond her for an instant and then back.

Susan's heart thudded within the cage of her chest. She took another step backward.

A growl like low thunder rumbled in the throat of the wolf. In one lithe bound, the great beast sprang from its lair. It hit the earth just in front of the woman, leaped again and landed in an all-out run. Like a phantom it vanished into the obscuring fall of sleet.

Susan shivered with relief. She must quickly get away from the den of the wolf. She spun around to retrace her steps.

A wavering, indistinct form rushed at her from the white wall of sleet. For an instant, she thought the wolf was returning. She cried out shrilly. Then her startled senses recognized the figure was that of a running man, crouched low and gripping a long skinning knife in his hand.

The man hurled himself upon Susan, slamming her to the ground, crushing her breath from her lungs with a whistling sound.

She struck at the man, realizing as she did that he was an Indian. That added to her fear. He blocked the blow easily with his hand.

She had lost her hat, and the man grabbed her by the hair and hoisted her up as he climbed erect. Susan hit at him quickly, her blow landing solidly on his face.

He shouted something at her in a language she did not understand and shook her fiercely back and forth by the hair. She thought her scalp was tearing loose from the skull. Trembling with weakness, fear and outrage, Susan stood before the Indian.

Swiftly, he bound her hands in front, leaving a couple of yards of rawhide dangling. He retrieved his rifle from where it had been leaned against a tree before the silent attack, then immediately grabbed the end of the thong and broke into a trot. Susan ran stumbling after him.

They halted briefly at her horse and he lifted her astride. Running strongly, he guided a course up the valley toward the high country.

Susan hunched her shoulders and huddled low over her pony. She turtled her neck low in her collar, seeking as much protection as possible from the hard sleet that assaulted every exposed inch of skin. The splinters of ice pounded her head and face and found entrance inside her clothing, where they melted to ice water and sent chill after shivery chill through her.

CHAPTER 15

The storm winds careened across the forested mountainside and whipped the pine trees like stems of grass. Billions of frozen raindrops plummeted downward, each tearing a hole through the frigid drafts to pelt the flanks of the ancient mountain.

Many of the swiftly falling spheres vanished without a trace into the turbulent water flow of the Niwot River. Others fell upon the lone horseman making his way through the late evening shadows on the bank of the river.

Luke only slowed for a moment when the tracks he followed disappeared under the crackling crust of sleet. He continued onward, convinced the outlaws were taking the trail to Gold Hill. That path, hollowed and eroded by the pounding of the iron-shod hooves of scores of miners' horses, was still discernible as it twisted and turned through the pine woods.

The route swerved away from the river and tilted to climb up over a massive jumble of angular boulders and earth where in some long-ago time a slab of the mountain had torn loose from the solid rock core and slid into the stream. The trail soon steepened more and Luke reined the black horse to a stop. He peered ahead into the storm.

All around, the forest was full of the sibilant strum of the falling sleet. The treetops swayed and tossed and the wind moaned as it was speared by the sharp edges of the pine needles. Here and there in the woods accumulations of the frozen moisture fell from unstable, thrashing branches with loud thumps upon the ground.

Above the sound of the storm Luke heard another noise below him in a shadow-filled canyon, the crash of the cold, heavy water of the Niwot tumbling and splashing down its rock-filled bed.

In front of him an unbroken ground sheet of sleet stretched up the steep grade. His horse could climb that slick and dangerous surface, but it would take time. There was something more important than further searching. He had to return to Susan before full darkness caught him. Insuring her safety was the most pressing task to perform this night. He turned the snow-covered horse back along the river channel.

Moments later an Indian on foot and leading a horse carrying a slumped figure upon its back came out of the trees and into the trail above where Coldiron had stopped. The Arapaho glanced down the stream and saw nothing except the downward-streaking sleet. He headed up the slope.

The sleet had changed to snow by the time Luke rode into the trees where Susan had been left. The flakes drifted in silently, piling up swiftly. Night was closing the woods in and only a feeble luminescence from the white ground covering held the darkness at bay.

"Susan! Susan, where are you?" Luke called out into the gloomy dusk of the pines.

No voice answered in reply.

He jumped from his horse and made a fast sweep around the area. There was not one imprint of Susan's footsteps in the two inches of snow and sleet.

He found the tarpaulin where he had tossed it on the ground. As he knocked the snow from it, a cold breeze ran up his spine and the short hair twisted on the back of his neck. The woman would not have failed to make the shelter. That would have been the very first thing she would do. If she was able.

Luke broke into a run, widening the circumference of his search, spiraling outward from the tarpaulin as a locus. Near the side of the valley where the land pitched abruptly upward, he found Susan's hat, full of snow.

The fear that he had lost her grew with a rush. Somehow the outlaws had doubled back past him and taken her. He considered the possibility that other men had captured her, but the odds of that were very slim. It must be the very men Susan and he had trailed so far to trap. Only to fall into their snare.

He did not want to believe she was gone, that if he should shout loudly enough, she would answer. However, he made not a sound for the signs were plain. She was gone.

Visibility had gradually lessened as he had scoured the forest. Now the darkness seemed to collapse upon him. Hastily, he made his way back to his horse.

The hungry and tired animal was tied to the tree near which it stood. "Sorry about there being no feed for you," Luke told the horse. The beast looked at him briefly, then dropped its head and humped its back against the snow and wind.

The canvas was again shaken free of snow, spread out, and folded once. Within the fold, Luke placed his bed. One layer of canvas would shelter him from the storm above and the other thickness from the snowy ground.

Luke stared out through the trees where the night lay cold as iron. In his mind's eye he saw Susan's haunting face and heard the echoes of her voice when she had told him, "Please wait and ask me again."

Would there be another opportunity, another time for them to be together? Vicious men had captured her. They could have greatly harmed her, maybe already killed her. Luke's fists balled into bony hammers. In the impenetrable blackness of this unknown land, there was absolutely nothing he could do now to find and rescue her.

The deepening cold penetrated Luke's clothing, and he crawled in under the canvas and into his sleeping robe. He hoped fervently that he could find Susan uninjured. He cursed himself for having left her alone and unprotected.

The black wintry night wrapped him in its snowy darkness. He lay hour after hour waiting for the first glimmer of daylight so he could find his enemies and with a blast of his gun send them both to hell.

The Arapaho forced the horse carrying the woman up the perilous, icy slope. At the top the tall form of Clason materialized from out of the storm to meet them.

"What have you there?" asked the white man in the Arapaho tongue, and moved up close to better see Susan.

"A good cayuse and a woman."

"I can see that. What happened?"

"Found her all alone. I thought at first she was a man, and I almost killed her. But she screamed and I heard the woman in her voice. That held my hand, for women are too valuable to destroy."

"It would have been a terrible waste to kill a woman so pretty," agreed Clason. "Did you look for sign of a man with her."

"Yes. It was snowing hard and I found nothing."

"There is a man close. No white woman would travel alone in these mountains. Follow me."

Clason hastily guided the way off the trail and to five horses in a small clearing. Grabbing up the reins and lead ropes, he led far back into thick pine and fir.

"Tie her there under that tree where the snow hasn't reached and let's go back to the trail," said Clason. "Whoever is with her may come looking and we'll take care of any problem he might cause."

Ghost Walker shoved Susan to the ground. He bound her hands behind her back and lashed her feet together.

"That will hold her," he said.

Silent as phantom hunters, the men faded into the murky snowfall.

Susan lay on the mat of needles beneath the low, sagging limbs of the giant fir tree and watched the men leave with their rifles. The instant they were out of sight, she began to tear at her bindings, straining every muscle to pull her hands free of the restraining knots.

With each desperate jerk, the rawhide thong cut more deeply into her flesh, clinching down so tightly she thought her wrists were being severed. She ceased the futile struggle and rested.

A spray of snow swirled in under the busy branches of the tree and settled on her. As she licked the flakes from her lips, she knew with sureness Luke could never locate her in the storm and darkness. Somehow she must get her feet loose and go find him.

She used all the strength of her legs to break the cord that hold her ankles. The binding gave not at all and she knew that somehow it must be untied.

By arching her body backwards and bringing her feet up, she was able to reach the thong that hold her legs. Her cold, numb fingers fumbled again and again with the hard knots. They would not loosen the slightest.

Exhausted, she huddled on the mat of needles and listened for the return of her captors. The wind snuffled along the ground and in among the trees and rocks like some great hunting beast. A frigid gust found her and laid its hand on every part of her body. Her jaws shook and she shivered against the arctic cold.

In the darkness the two men returned through the forest like night-seeing animals. Without a word, they hunkered over her. Susan remained very still, sighting up at their indistinct forms.

Clason touched her face. "She's like ice. Her gear is on her horse. Let's fix her a warm bed. I don't want her to die."

"We are safe here, for no one can find us in the snow," said Ghost Walker. "I will build a fire to warm her."

"Good. I'd like to get a better look at what we have caught. I don't have any matches. Can you start a fire with flint and steel in all this wind?"

"This is only a little wind. Out on the broad, flat plain in the wintertime, that is where the invisible part of the world truly moves swiftly. Even there I can build a fire with my spark maker."

Ghost Walker felt around on the blanket of needles and broken twigs that had rained down from the tall tree and selected certain objects by touch. He drew from inside his painted shirt the pouch containing the flint and steel, a few pieces of punk and twists of fine grass.

Leaning close to the trunk of the fir to shield his effort from the wind, he skillfully struck the flint upon the roughened strip of steel. A little burst of sparks exploded into life to rain down upon a segment of the punk pressed firmly into one of the twists of grass.

"Ah! It catches and burns," said the Arapaho as he waved the punk and grass in an arc through the air. A red ember glowed softly in the blackness.

He placed the success of his handiwork between two of the spreading roots of the tree. Flames were soon flickering and growing as he added fuel.

Clason unbound Susan's hands. "Go to the fire," he told her. "But do not touch the ties that hold your feet. I do not want to have to chase you through the woods."

Susan scooted herself near the leaping flames. The warmth was like a tonic and she breathed deeply of it. Her body made one last shaking shiver and began to warm.

Ghost Walker went to the horses and returned with her blanket roll. He dropped it beside her and stepped across the fire to lean against the fir tree.

Susan pulled the bundle to her and in surprise found one additional blanket with it. The Indian must have given her one of his.

She untied the blankets and laid aside the personal items contained inside. The blankets were spread one upon another to form a thick covering. Sitting on the edge of the blankets, Susan drew the remainder up over her back and around her head. The front was left open to receive the heat radiating out from the fire.

The black-bearded white man squatted with his hands out to the flames. He was dressed in heavy wool trousers and coat, and a broadbrimmed felt hat. A fringe of buckskin showed at his wrists, as if he had donned the wool outfit over clothing already being worn. Through narrow slit eyes he inspected Susan in a sly and calculating way.

Susan faced away from Clason and toward the Indian. Quick black eyes like those of a hawk were watching her.

He wore buckskin trousers and shirt, with a second buckskin shirt, very much like her own, as a piece of outerwear. A cap of wolfskin covered his head. His clothing was skimpy and there was snow in the tangles of his long black hair; however, the glacial cold did not appear to bother him.

The Arapaho sank down to the ground, stretched, then relaxed beside the fire like a lean brown dog.

"Where are your menfolk?" Clason questioned Susan.

"At Gold Hill," responded Susan.

"Are you traveling alone?"

"Yes. I came up from Denver to meet my husband at the

gold camp. He is expecting me and I should have been there by now."

"You are a liar. No man would let his woman ride forty miles alone in this Indian country."

"I've told you the truth," lied Susan.

Clason laughed. "She says her man is up at Gold Hill," he said to Ghost Walker.

"Maybe she speaks the truth, for I did not see sign of anyone," said Ghost Walker.

"Not on your life," retorted Clason. He switched back to English and spoke to Susan. "You are not a good liar. I'd bet everything I own that your man was within a mile or so of you when the Indian found you."

"Believe what you want," said Susan. Her mouth closed firmly and she looked into the fire. She would answer no more questions.

Clason studied Susan's stern features. "What is your name?"

Susan did not reply. Clason saw her muscles tense, as if she expected to be struck.

"Fact is, it doesn't make much difference whether or not you are riding alone or what your name is. We're going to be damn careful and we'll be ready for any trouble that comes our direction."

Clason chuckled as he pitched a chunk of wood on the fire. Everything was working out fine. His eyes moved between the Arapaho and the woman. In Missouri he had thought it was bad luck that the pretty blond woman could not make the journey to the mountains with him. However, that original plan was not dead, only altered.

This black-haired woman, even more beautiful than the first, had fallen easily into his hands. The Indian be damned. Clason would take her and all the gold.

Clason chuckled as he contemplated the future months and a much longer time to come. He had built a solid cabin up high in the mountains on a tributary of the South Platte River. For three years he had trapped for ermine and wolf there. It would be a snug place to spend the winter. Then in the spring the woman and he would ride far south into the New Mexico Territory. With his large sum of gold a magnificent rancho could be created in that broad land.

The world was a damn fine place to live.

Ghost Walker kept his expression impassive as he looked across the fire and into the cunning blue eyes of Clason. The man had just made an important resolution, like the time out on the prairie when they had talked of the wolves and decided to rob the white men of their gold. The Arapaho believed this last decision had much to do with the woman and so for certain with the gold. Constant guard must be maintained to protect himself from Clason, for only the quest for gold cemented the bond between them. When that binding force broke, they would fight to the death.

"Time to eat," said Clason. He rummaged in the packs and returned with two pouches. "Dried apples in this one and buffalo jerky in the other. Help yourself. Don't wait for the Indian; he doesn't eat a hell of a lot."

Susan reached to retrieve a handful of the slices of apples. She lowered her head quickly, for her heart was suddenly racing and she did not want the men to detect that she had recognized the sack of fruit as part of the stores she had purchased in Denver. She knew without the slightest doubt that these men were the ones who had slain Dan and Phil. Their gold would be in the packs lying on the ground near the horses.

She chewed slowly on the leathery fruit, not tasting the sweetness at all. The cold no longer existed for her, nor the fire. Only these two horrible men. If she had a weapon, she would shoot them both dead without the least compunction for the killing.

Ghost Walker came around the fire and took some of the apples and jerky. He saw the woman's face tense with some emotion she was striving to hide. He felt a tinge of regret for having captured her. The deed was done. A new path had been opened for Clason and himself to follow. He retreated to his original space and began to eat.

Clason secured some of the food and found a seat. His smile had vanished under a bleak expression.

The flames gradually grew short as the wood was consumed. Susan cautiously moved her vision to intently inspect the bearded white man and the leanly sinewed Indian in the dying blaze. The wind poked in under the tree to flutter the fire, and the alternating flit of shadow and flare of flame in the hollows and crevices of their hard faces made them appear like evil ghosts. Oh, how she wished them both dead.

The Arapaho lifted his hand and pointed past Clason. A pair of eyes burned red in the darkness just beyond the reach of the light of the fire.

"Wolf," said Clason.

"My brother the wolf," agreed Ghost Walker.

"That means no other human is near. We can sleep sound tonight," said Clason. He looked at Susan and laughed.

CHAPTER 16

Coldiron crawled from the snow-covered bed and packed the horse. The darkness faded as he worked, and a brittle polar morning came to life.

The wind lay quiet. The snow had ceased. Six inches of white blanketed the ground, and the trunks of the trees were plastered with snow on the windward side.

Overhead clouds hung against the mountain. A thin sliver of dusky gray sky showed on the bare eastern horizon.

With snow crunching under his boots, Luke went in the direction of the trail. He had gone only a short way when dark forms appeared among the trees and a herd of fifteen or so elk—cows, calves, and two bulls—came into sight. Their breath plumed out like tiny clouds of floating silver as they glanced nervously over their shoulders trying to identify the thing that had spooked them.

One of the bulls raised his muzzle, laid his massive antlers over his back and fled through the trees in a series of long, lithe bounds. The other elk followed, throwing clods of snow from their driving hooves. They passed a hundred paces in front of the man and disappeared into a dense stand of ponderosas.

Luke continued ahead to the elk's path. As he sighted along the stretch of disturbed snow, the course of a game trail could be discerned. He guided his horse onto that age-old way and went in the opposite direction from that taken by the elk. No one, without looking very closely, could detect his horse's tracks among the many hoofprints already there.

The route crossed the man-made trail to Gold Hill and went toward the Niwot. The path turned and climbed steeply up the mountain along the rim of the gorge.

Below Luke the river raced its raging, turbulent passage through the chaos of rock nearly blocking the fifty-foot bed. Submerged boulders shunted the flow of water violently upward to create tall waves upon the bosom of the stream and large stringers of foam streaked past, fast as a man could run. Sprays of water arched in long white horsetails. Every splash upon a rock left behind a coating of ice.

The gray wedge of sky in the east grew a yellow tinge as the sun fought upward from its nighttime bedding place. The rim of the golden sun crested the curve of the earth and a dazzling shaft of light flashed over the flat plain and struck the mountainside.

Coldiron saw movement on the lip of the ravine at the top of the hill. Caught in the sparkling sunlight and silhouetted on the white snow were three human forms. One of them struck a swift blow. A counterstrike was returned equally fast. A distant, deadly battle was being fought.

Out of the mix of figures, one tumbled from the rim of the gorge, rotating slowly as it fell. Luke recognized the brightly colored Indian shirt worn by Susan, and her long black hair streaming in the air.

The falling body hit a slanting ledge of rock partway down the canyon wall, glanced from it, spinning rapidly. The form barely missed a granite boulder rimmed with ice and plummeted out of sight in the cascading water.

Luke's heart shifted within him and his breath left in a thin whistle of pain. Dumbstruck at the sudden, horrible event, he stood immobile for a moment.

He dropped the reins of the horse and spun to run back along the rim of the canyon. Susan had fallen a long, bone-breaking distance. Yet by some miracle, she might still be alive. She must be gotten quickly from the river before she drowned or froze in the frigid water.

Where the rim was broken and brush and rock had created a steeply sloping descent to the river, Luke plunged downward. Clutching at the stems of the shrubs and clambering

over the rocks, he partly fell and partly slid to the bottom.
Immediately, he scrambled up the stream in the direction of
the place where Susan had fallen.

He ran, sometimes on the shore, but more often in the
shallow edge of the speeding river to avoid rocks blocking his
way. The canyon was choked with deafening noise. The very
earth shook with the crash and fall of the stupendous volume
of water. Susan could be calling him from a few feet away
and he would not be able to hear her. He cast his eyes swiftly
around.

In a patch of foam rushing by in the current, a forked stick
of wood, rubbed free of bark and the color of flesh, waggled
at him like a hand beckoning. Luke threw a curse at it for the
momentary speeding of his heart it had caused.

He stepped into the river to go around a large angular stone
that had tumbled down from the rim. As he waded, the water
rose to his waist and the awesome strength of the current
clutched at him. He grabbed hold of the rock to keep from
being dragged from his feet and worked his way to the bank.
His body began to shiver from the immersion in the frigid
water, and he hurried faster.

If Susan had been swept into the deeper main current, there
was little likelihood that she would be able to escape it. She
would be battered upon the rocks by thousands of tons of
water and washed miles downstream. Luke shoved that dread-
ful thought away.

He found the location where he thought Susan had fallen.
He sighted up at the rim and decided she had landed in or
near a deep, swirling eddy close to the base of the canyon
wall. He inspected the rotating pool of water and the mass of
foam, pine needles and pieces of broken tree limbs being
carried endlessly round and round.

There was no sign of her. Only the shredded fragments of
once-whole trees.

Luke ran to the first cluster of boulders downstream from
the pool. Susan might be trapped there, caught against the
rock and held by the current. He searched among them.
Nothing was there except the water and the rocks with their
thick skirts of ice.

The minutes fled by as Luke hastened beside the river. His
eyes jumped from one side of the stream to the other, scouring

every pool of water, the jumbles of driftwood wedged on the boulders, and the infrequent gravel bars.

He continued downstream, passing beyond the point of his descent to the river bottom. With each step his hopes of finding Susan dwindled.

Luke discovered the broken and frozen body of a large buck deer, impaled on the spearlike shafts of driftwood wedged between rocks. Even that powerful animal had fallen victim to the mighty Niwot.

The day wore on and Luke combed the river for miles. Finally, he turned back, searching the very same area a second time. The river must not be allowed to claim her permanently. She must be found and given a proper burial in the earth.

The daylight grew dim, fading to dusk. Luke stopped in consternation at the failing light. He looked up at the overcast sky. The entire day was spent and the search must end. His race to save Susan from the freezing water was lost. He turned about and sadly made his way downstream toward the faintly seen sloping pile of rock that marked the ascent out of the canyon.

In a narrow section of shoreline, a boulder extended from the wall of the gorge and out into the river to block his course. As Luke climbed up to pass over the obstacle, he slipped on a spot of ice and fell. In an instant he was sliding down the face of the rock. He dropped into the strong flow of the river and the water closed over him.

The current held him submerged, rolling and spinning him. Never had he experienced anything so cold. As if the river had stored a hundred winters in its depths.

The warmth and elasticity of his muscles washed away with the onslaught of the water. In an instant his muscles began to stiffen.

He was rammed against a boulder on the bottom of the river. Frantically, he kicked upward from it. His head broke the surface and his lungs sucked starvingly at the life-giving air.

He flailed to stay on top, fighting the turbulent water that pulled mightily to draw him down. He saw the shore and stroked fiercely to break free of the current.

One second he was in water hurtling downstream at a

dizzying speed, then a foot closer to the bank he broke into a circling eddy behind a giant boulder. The reverse current caught him and carried him upstream. Dirty foam and forest trash closed around him. He was transported three times around that stagnant vortex before his feet touched the bottom and he crawled upon the bank.

Luke climbed erect and began to walk. To falter or hesitate to rest would mean his death. Warmth must be found within minutes, and the only source was his buffalo sleeping robe on his horse somewhere on the top of the canyon.

His clothes began to freeze in less than a minute. In three, they were solid ice, like armor. The only places that would bend were at the continually moving joints of his arms and legs.

The energy store of his body rapidly diminished as the cold drove inward. His mind was growing numb and he sensed the befuddlement at the fringe of his thoughts.

The break in the canyon wall was reached and he began the long climb out. The tortuous ascent seemed unending. Finally, he staggered up the last step and stood on the rim of the gorge.

The black horse was hungry. While it had waited patiently for the return of its master, it pawed in the snow trying to uncover some of the scant sprigs of grass that grew in the woods.

A weak call sounded from down the hill and the horse twisted to look. It saw its master stumbling about, going a few paces first in one direction and then another in a dazed way on the edge of the canyon.

The man cried out again in a plaintive voice. The cayuse recognized the urgency in the feeble command and went obediently to see what was wanted.

Luke leaned on the horse and gathered his failing strength for one last critical effort. He reached for the leather thong that fastened the rolled tarpaulin and his sleeping robe to the back of the horse. His fumbling fingers at first refused to grasp the end of the tie. At last, they caught the binding and tugged the knot loose. He then circled the horse and worked the second tie off. The canvas and its contents tumbled to the snowy ground.

With stiff, unfeeling hands, Luke poked and pounded at the canvas until it lay spread upon the snow. The fur robe unfolded more easily. His clothes seemed to require an impossible length of time to remove. He noted with surprise that the six-gun was still in the holster, held there by the loop over the heel of the hammer.

Naked and nearly immobile, Luke wrapped the thick buffalo robe around him and pulled the canvas over the top. His body fought its last defense against the cold, shivering and shaking to generate life-sustaining warmth within the muscles. The violence of the action seemed ready to wrench every tendon loose from its anchoring points on his bones.

Coldiron did not know when he lapsed into unconsciousness.

Susan slept in all her clothes and wrapped in the blankets. The men rested in their fur robes beside her, one on each side. Every time she stirred to seek a more comfortable position, she sensed them come awake and alert.

Her sleep was shallow, for the deep cold awoke her often. The men in their thick buffalo hides seemed to slumber warmly. She was awake when they arose.

"Time to get up," the white man said.

Susan felt the nudge of his toe in her ribs. "Where are we going?" she questioned.

"That's not important to you now. You will know when you get there."

Susan felt her anger rise, but held her sharp retort and looked around. It was barely light enough to see in the deep woods. The snow had halted, but not before an inch had drifted in under the fir tree. She brushed it from her possessions and rolled them in the blankets.

The men hastened to saddle the riding mounts and load the packs on the other horses. Finishing that, they gathered the gear scattered about. The white man came past Susan with the pouches of jerky and dried apples.

"Eat," he directed brusquely, holding out the two open containers.

Susan took a large handful from each and shoved the food into a pocket. The men would relax their guard on her sooner or later and she would slip away and escape. Until that time, she must do all that was possible to prepare for it.

Clason did not move on; instead, he looked keenly into her face as if trying to read her thoughts. He pulled reflectively at his beard, grunted and walked toward the horses.

With Susan in the center, the cavalcade of horses and riders came to the border of the forest. Clason motioned a stop, and both men dismounted and went forward to examine the trail that stretched close to the wall of the river gorge. Susan climbed down from her pony. She could see that the snow lay without imprint on all sides.

The men began to converse in the language of the Indian. Susan could not guess of what they spoke, but their hands moved in quick accents to the statements and she knew they disagreed.

The Indian pointed up the mountain toward Gold Hill and the white man shook his head. The Indian then indicated one of the heavily laden pack animals. Susan heard the word "gold," followed by a rapid discourse. The white man spread his hands wide and spoke in a mollifying tone.

The hungry horses gathered around a nearby bushy aspen tree and started to bite at the tender tips of the limbs. They chewed noisily and stomped the ground, and pushed and shoved each other to reach the food.

Near Susan a length of pine wood, a broken limb some four feet long and as large in diameter as her lower arm, partially protruded from the snow. Watching the men carefully, she drew the stick to her. The wood saturated by the rains that had washed the mountains before becoming snow, and now frozen solid, was as heavy and hard as iron.

With her footsteps masked by the noise of the feeding horses, Susan stole upon the arguing men. They stood within a pace of each other. A downward-shelving rock ledge, slick with snow, separated them from the canyon.

Susan gripped the club. Damn the killers to hell. She would knock both of them into the river.

Sunlight suddenly flooded the mountainside. In the clearing where lay the trail, the pristine snow sparkled. The beam of light was upon Clason's back and into the face of Ghost Walker.

The men were engrossed in their dispute and stood wary of a quick attack by the other with knife or rifle. The stalking approach of the woman was not observed.

Susan came out of the shadows of the woods with the club drawn far back, tensed for a powerful roundhouse swing. The last few feet she rushed at the two men. She was within two strides of them before they heard her running steps and whirled to look.

Clason saw the danger immediately. Ghost Walker, with the sun in his eyes, saw only an outline form. He lifted a hand to block the bright rays.

Susan swung the cudgel, pivoting with it, exerting every ounce of her strength. With an ever increasing speed, the heavy piece of wood cut a flat arc in the air.

Clason ducked and the accelerating club missed his head, catching his hat to send it sailing.

The hard pine limb continued its path. It beat aside Ghost Walker's upraised hand and slammed savagely into his face. He was hammered backwards, slid on the sloping ledge and toppled into the canyon.

Above the vibrations radiating up the length of the wood, Susan had felt the cheekbones and forehead of the Indian crush. Swiftly, she drew the club back and struck downward at an angle at the crouching white man.

Clason dove at the woman's legs, trying to get in under the blow. As he fell, he thrust the barrel of his rifle at her.

The ramming steel cylinder speared the center of Susan's chest. The wicked strike sent shock waves of excruciating pain pounding at the base of her brain. She thought the man had shot her.

Her hands lost their strength and the club slipped from her grip. She sagged to her knees. Instantly, Clason sprang on her, bowling her over in the snow. He flopped her face up and dropped astride of her. His thighs penned her arms.

"Goddamn you!" thundered Clason. "You tried to kill me." He slapped her ruthlessly left and right with his bony hands.

Flashes of fire burned a course through Susan's already battered brain. She tensed for the hard hands to strike her again.

The blows did not come. She waited. Her eyes opened a thin crack to look at the hated enemy. He was staring at the edge of the canyon where the Indian had fallen from sight.

Clason began to smile. The smile worked its way up to a chuckle.

"You killed the Arapaho for me. I would have had to do that sooner or later." Clason clamped Susan's face between thumb and fingers and glared down at her. "And you would've knocked my head off too if I hadn't been watching."

Clason sat on Susan and continued to hold her face. She watched the cunning eyes and the rapid play of thought behind them. He tugged at his long black beard with his free hand.

"You're a killer and could be downright dangerous to a man. But you're a damn fine-looking woman and worth a little risk to own. Now that I know what you are, I'll be careful not to give you a second chance at me."

He jerked a piece of rawhide from a pocket and bound her hands. "Come on." He dragged her erect and led her to the mounts.

"Get on the horse." He hoisted her up under the arms and swung her astride.

Roughly, he caught her by the knee and squeezed. "You are a handsome woman, but if you try to hurt me again, I'll kill you quick. Do you understand me?"

Susan's head buzzed and the world was spinning dizzily around her. Her chest ached as if it had been crushed. She heard the man's voice, but the meaning of his words did not register.

She took hold of the pommel of the saddle and held on tightly. The dizziness left her, but the pain persisted. The man still spoke. She did not listen. Instead, she looked out over the gorge of the Niwot to the far snowy wall.

Under her breath, she repeated the vow made to Dan and Phil those many days ago: "I will kill without mercy or warning as they did to you."

Clason turned from the woman and surveyed the trail to Gold Hill. This last snow would surely drive even the heartiest of the miners down from the mountains. They could reach this point by late in the day or early on the morrow. He was in a good position to easily waylay some of them and take their gold.

He reflected upon the idea. Now with the Indian dead, he did not need additional gold so badly as to delay here longer.

He tied the packhorses nose to tail and took up the lead

rope of the head animal. He swung up on the back of his mount, and leaving Ghost Walker's cayuse standing in the grove of aspen, led off swiftly down the winding trail.

The tracks of the herd of elk were encountered and Clason and Susan rode off on top of them for a way. When the track veered steeply to the left, he steered directly down the flank of the mountain.

The wind built, driving from the north. It pressed the clouds against the mountains, squeezing hard round balls of sleet from them. They fell like spent pellets from a shotgun upon the man and woman.

Clason increased the pace. In three days' time, four at the most, he would be at his cabin far up on a tributary of the South Platte River. The gold was his. So too was the woman. The mountains would be deserted. Ah! It would be a fine, enjoyable winter.

CHAPTER 17

Luke surfaced from the deep sleep of exhaustion and lay without moving under the canvas. The familiar odor of the buffalo robe was in his nostrils and he felt the coarse hair against his naked skin. The rumble of the Niwot River in the bottom of the gorge was a distant thunder.

At the thought of the river all the sadness of Susan's death welled up unbidden within him. He relived her fall from the canyon rim, saw her body strike the rock with bone-crushing force and vanish into the cold waters. She was dead. He had tested the killing strength of the river and knew no human, even uninjured, could survive it but for a very few minutes.

She had accompanied him for only a short time. Still, he could recall every curve of her face and all the feminine movements that had given him such deep pleasure. Just once had he touched her, and then for the briefest of moments. However, those days with her had cut a hard grove in the memory of his mind, one that would never be eroded away by time.

Luke had never felt so lonely, so incomplete, and he knew it was because the woman was gone. He keenly sensed that his old solitary life had left something out. There was an elemental knowledge at the center of his consciousness that he needed her above all things.

Something touched the canvas above Luke's face. He lifted up on the covering, and from its weight, knew more snow had fallen. Gingerly, so that none of it would fall into his bed, he folded back the canvas.

The gaunt black horse stood over him, ears down, head sagging, and one hind foot drawn up on its edge. Its ribs were beginning to show painfully. Large brown eyes examined Coldiron questioningly.

He reached out and rubbed the soft muzzle. "Old fellow, did you think I might be dead like your first master?" he asked the pony.

The horse nickered a friendly response and tossed its head in pleasure. Then it lowered its head again and nuzzled close to coax more petting strokes from the man.

Luke obliged the faithful horse. He was glad for its company. For some unexplainable reason, the cayuse of the slain Indian had transferred all its loyalty to him.

Snow was falling steadily and a foot or more hid the earth. The day was exceptionally dim. Luke had lost all track of time and he wondered if it was morning or evening. Had he slept one night or on through the day?

He climbed out of his bed to stand naked in the snowfall. Every muscle in his body felt bruised and strained. The tenderness in his toes informed him the boundary of frostbite had been reached and passed. The soreness would take days to heal.

Luke looked quickly out through the woods. No wind stirred, and the snow fell in white streaks from the darkening sky. The thick boles of the pine and fir stood black and somber. No living thing moved in the scope of his vision. The mountain was caught fast in winter.

He stepped around the horse and to the pack upon its back. He dug out the clothing that had belonged to one of the dead men of Susan's party. Had the articles been worn by her husband? No matter. Luke desperately needed them. His own were a pile of ice somewhere under the white drifts.

The snow was brushed from his body and he donned the warm, dry garments. Looking up, he inspected the weak light working its way down through the clouds and snowflakes. The dusk was deepening and he realized it was evening and the day was ending.

Walking barefoot in the snow, Coldiron unpacked the horse, removed the saddle and tethered the lean beast on the end of a rope. The hungry horse had remained with him until now. However, its hunger would grow more intense, for the scant grass of the forest was now buried. The mount was vital to Luke's survival and he must not gamble on its straying off.

He found the clothing that had gone into the river with him. After beating some of the ice from the garments on the trunk of a tree, he hung the articles over a limb.

He compressed a mass of snow in his hands and ate it. A quarter pound of raisins was extracted from the store of food in the pack. Chewing slowly, one sweet raisin at a time, he savored the delicious flavor.

The bite of snow on Luke's feet became painful. He shook the accumulation of white from his head and clothing. Taking his frozen boots and his six-gun with him so they would thaw, he slid back into the bed.

Tomorrow the search for Susan's body would continue. She deserved a burial in the earth and not to be left to the claws and beaks of the scavengers of land and air.

In the sunlight of early morning, the black horse and its rider made their way along the canyon of the Niwot. Coldiron intently scrutinized down into the gorge full of the clamor of the river roaring over its bed of boulders. He still hoped to give Susan proper internment. He would build a large stone monument to mark the grave.

A mile passed, then another, and the walls of the canyon shrank in height. They drew back from the Niwot and the stream widened and slowed its hectic pace.

Beneath the long, outstretched limbs of a dense fir, Luke discovered the tracks of several horses. He stepped down from his saddle and carefully evaluated the indentations.

Strong winds had ushered in the snowstorm two days before. An inch or so of snow had been blown in under the fir to blanket the ground. The storm front had drawn the winds with it as it had pushed onward. The snow that followed had fallen vertically to accumulate on the branches and leave undisturbed the skiff beneath the tree.

Coldiron counted the tracks of five horses. Plainly visible was the sign of the marker horses, the one with the end of its right front shoe broken and the second animal with the small hooves.

The tracks could be followed no farther than the edge of the tree. Beyond that border the deep snow hid the impressions. Luke sighted along the course of the horses. The outlaws were heading down from the mountains to the grasslands of the prairie.

Luke continued traveling beside the river. Miles now separated him from the place Susan had fallen. She was lost forever from him. There would be no monument of stone.

However, there was a greater monument, the mighty Niwot River would for time unending remind him of her.

The horse was guided away from the river and directly down the slope of the mountain. The hungry animal stepped out eagerly. It seemed to know the course would lead to the abundant grass on the plain.

The foothills were left behind and Luke came out onto the flat, snow-cloaked prairie. He veered north. He sill intended to locate the trail of the outlaws. To do that he must find tracks made after the storm of the past night had stopped.

For two hours the horse waded the deep snow. Many fresh trails were intercepted. Some were of deer and elk migrating from the cold mountains to the warmer low country. Others were made by the unshod hooves of wild mustangs wandering here and there as they fed.

He reversed his route, retracing the tough miles made to the north, and continued south. He found nothing to indicate that the outlaws had passed that way. Their path was hidden somewhere under the heavy snow.

The Niwot River, now slow and placid, was encountered about twenty miles upstream from where it rendezvoused with the South Platte River. Coldiron searched the twists and bends of the Niwot until a ford was found shallow enough to wade. Beyond the river a course was set straight for Denver.

Night caught Luke before he reached Denver. The darkness deepened and a cold, white moon rose to glare grimly down from the black winter sky. The horse labored through the snow, breathing hard and noisily in its weariness.

Luke halted on the top of a rise outside the city. He sat his mount in the lonely gloom and ranged his eyes over the town.

The cold wind sighed sadly as it came across the snow from Denver. The lines of square hulks of buildings were black night shadows on the moonlit snowscape. Scores of windows glowed dull yellow from the flames of coal-oil lamps.

Faint, distant voices and laughter and the music of fiddle strings drifted on the air. A gunshot exploded somewhere in the town. All sound ceased as if waiting to see if there would be a second shot. After a few seconds the human racket swiftly rebuilt its volume to the original crescendo.

The cluster of buildings and the people held no attraction for Coldiron except as a source of food and shelter. He would spend one night there and then leave to return to his ranch in the New Mexico Territory.

He rode down from the hill to the town and went along Blake Street. At the first livery stable he pushed open the big wooden door and entered. A lighted lantern turned low dimly illuminated the interior. He called out for the stableman. Only his own voice echoed back.

The horse was led into a vacant stall and given an armload of hay. From a burlap sack of oats, Luke dipped out a large measure with a gallon tin can and poured it into the feedbox in the corner of the horse's manger. Silently promising the stalwart mount a good brushing of his coat on the morrow, Luke closed the stable door and left.

The music of a piano and fiddle drifted from a two-story, wood-frame building on Luke's side of the street. The clap of hands and stomp of feet told of a fast dance in progress. Fingering the thin five-dollar gold piece the robbers had missed, Luke wearily shoved open the door of the Criterion Hall Saloon and went inside.

The establishment was one extremely large room. A long mahogany bar was to the left. A dance platform was on his right.

A hundred men—miners, cowboys and teamsters in coarse clothing—packed the high-ceilinged room. Here and there a townsman was conspicuous in a suit with a white shirt. A score of women all wearing brightly colored, short-skirted outfits mingled with the men. Most of the women were on the dance floor with a male partner. Luke paid no attention to the crowd except to glance at the swiftly moving couples swinging to the music.

The dance ended as he leaned against the bar and sipped at

his first whiskey. Some of the dancers made their way back to their tables. Other pairs split apart, the women winding through the all-male patrons to cadge a drink from a lonesome man and earn a commission. Several men and women came to the bar.

Luke felt the unfamiliar press of their bodies and did not like the nearess. He drank the last of his whiskey and turned, intending to go past the end of the bar to where a man was eating at one of two small tables. Serving food was not a major undertaking in the Criterion.

"If you buy me a drink, I'll dance with you," said a woman's voice at his elbow.

The woman was tall, slightly thin, and her face was heavily painted with rouge and powder. The smell of whiskey was strong on her breath. She stared brazenly at Luke and took hold of his hand to squeeze between hers.

"I'm not looking for company," Luke said, and tried to withdraw his hand.

She clutched it more firmly and pressed it to her bosom. "I would think a big, strong man like you must need plenty of entertainment."

Coldiron could not help but contemplate the difference between the woman and Susan. The saloon woman did not compare favorably. He twisted his hand free. "I'm not interested. Go find someone else."

The woman's face hardened. She had understood the expression on Luke's countenance. "So you think I'm not good enough for you."

Luke's tiredness allowed his aggravation at the woman to grow. He took her by the shoulders, turned her about and guided her close to the man standing next along the bar. "This fellow looks like he wants to dance."

"Don't shove me around, you bastard," snarled the woman. She slapped at him.

Luke blocked the blow and stepped back. The woman was drunk and he wanted no trouble with her. "Let's call it even. If I've insulted you, I'm sorry."

His expression of apology set the woman into a frenzy of anger. She sprang at him, striking with both hands. "You son of a bitch," she shrieked, "I'm as good as you are."

Coldiron moved back out of her reach.

The woman started to advance upon Luke when a man caught her and quickly subdued her arms. "Easy, Dolly. Now just be quiet. I'll take care of this for you. Go over to that table and sit down."

Dolly glanced over her shoulder at the man and nodded. "All right, Frankie. But you're not going to let him insult me and push me around are you?"

"Certainly not. Now do as I say."

Dolly pivoted and stalked with stiff-legged stride to the table. The man faced Coldiron.

He stood slightly above average height and was muscular. His face was handsome, with a short, brown beard. He wore a dark wool suit, white shirt and black string tie.

"My name is Frankie Harrison. I own Criterion Hall. That woman and all the others here work for me. Dolly was just being friendly like she is paid to do. Why did you abuse her?"

Coldiron had seen Harrison around Denver and had heard the tales surrounding the man and his saloon. He was reported to have come from Georgia and to be a tough fellow. His gambling and drinking house was the hangout of most of the bullyboys, rogues and scoundrels of the Territory. It was believed by many people that Harrison organized and financed some of the robberies in and around Denver. A large number of the men standing and watching expectantly could be in his pay. Even if that was so, Coldiron was glad to be dealing with Harrison instead of the woman called Dolly.

"I didn't hurt her," said Coldiron. "She made me an offer that I did not want. Then started hitting at me when I told her to talk to that man standing there." As Coldiron spoke, he stepped a couple of paces closer to Harrison.

"He hurt me, Frankie," screamed the woman.

"Mister, I'm going to have to make you pay Dolly for the rough treatment you gave her. I'd say ten dollars in gold would settle the account."

Coldiron rubbed his chin as if thoughtfully considering the saloonkeeper's demand and eased another step nearer. Harrison could not back down in public before his cronies. There was no way to end this confrontation without a fight. Luke would have to use his fist, for his pistol had gone into the water of the Niwot River with him and every cartridge could be wet and not fire.

"Well, let's see how much money I've got," said Coldiron, and drew from his pocket the change remaining from the five dollars after the shot of whiskey had been purchased. As Coldiron counted the coins, he once again went forward a step.

Harrison's expression stiffened with suspicion. His hand brushed back the tail of his coat to expose a six-gun in a holster.

Coldiron grinned at him. "Not enough money here to pay it all. I guess I'll pay you this way." With a flick of his wrist, Coldiron flung the hard coins into Harrison's face and lunged at him.

The man blinked and his head flinched to the side, wasting a tiny sliver of a second before his hand streaked for his pistol.

Coldiron finished his leap and caught the saloonkeeper's gun hand just as he started to lift the weapon from its holster. Coldiron's right fist smashed savagely into Harrison's jaw, pummeling him backward.

Harrison pulled mightily with his hand to draw the six-gun. Coldiron held his grip on the man's wrist and slugged him in the side of the head. Harrison went limp and fell heavily to the dirt floor.

A rifle shot exploded in the confined space of the room. The flames in the coal-oil lamps danced and flickered at the concussion. All sound ceased abruptly.

"Everybody stand perfectly still," shouted a man in fierce warning. "I shot that man in the shoulder. I could've killed him easy. I will the next man that touches a gun."

Luke spun around. Lafe Pertusset and his three sons stood with their rifles raised near the front entrance. Luke twisted further, following Pertusset's line of sight and saw a man leaning against the wall holding his shoulder. Pain distorted his face and blood leaked between the fingers clutching at a wound.

Lafe Pertusset called out through the silence that lay in the saloon.

"Coldiron, come over here among friends before someone else tries to shoot you in the back."

For a moment every man and woman remained unmoving. Then a chair squeaked in the back of the room as a man climbed up on it to see over the heads of those standing in front obstructing his view.

"Do something, Frankie," Dolly yelled at Harrison, who was groggily rising up from the floor.

"Shut your damn mouth, you drunken bitch," roared Harrison. He struggled upright.

Luke went quickly to the side of the Pertussets. "I'm right glad to see you fellows," said Luke.

"I couldn't let him shoot you, not after what we owe you for the horse," responded Lafe.

"Never was a better time to pay a debt."

Grumbling voices began to sound. A man from somewhere in the center of the crowd shouted, "Harrison deserves our help."

"Best we slide out of here before his friends get their courage up," said Lafe.

"Good advice," answered Luke.

Lafe spoke over his shoulders to his sons. "Move! Out the door, all of you."

The elder Pertusset ranged his sight over the throng of men in the room. "I'll be outside. Any man that sticks his nose out the door inside two minutes will get it shot off."

Watching warily, Coldiron and Pertusset sidled swiftly through the door.

"This way. Hurry," directed Lafe, and ran along Blake Street. At the first cross street he guided left and increased his pace to a pounding run. He turned right at the next intersection and slowed to a walk.

"Do you think they will come after us?" Lafe questioned Luke.

"No. They'll talk about doing that, but won't come outside in the dark and risk getting shot. They'll go back to drinking for a while. Then some of Harrison's best gunhands will come out and scout around town and try to find out who we are. You had better stay out of sight for a while. Without a doubt, Harrison will try to get even."

"Well, that's all right. Me and my sons don't usually associate with folks like that. However, we found a pocket of gold up on the South Platte River. Got it dug out the day before the snow came. We were just coming into the saloon to have a drink and celebrate when we saw the trouble you were in.''

''Your luck is running strong to make a strike so soon,'' said Luke.

''Only a small pocket we dug out and washed in one day. About thirty ounces. Enough for us to winter on.'' Lafe looked intently at Coldiron. ''You once told me you could pull that handgun mighty fast. Now why didn't you shoot that mean rascal in the saloon?''

''Because I fell in the river with it on. The powder in every shell could be soaked with water. If I had drawn my pistol and it misfired, Harrison would've shot me dead.''

''That was a mighty long gamble to walk up to him and knock him on his ass,'' said Lafe.

''I'm much obliged to all of you for your help,'' said Luke. ''You have made a bad enemy in Harrison. Watch out for him.''

''We're not afraid of him,'' said Denzele from the shadows. ''If he comes after us, we'll show him some Kentucky fighting.''

Coldiron heard the other brothers chuckle. The Pertussets would be a tough clan to start a war with.

''How is your dad,'' asked Luke.

''Healing right fine,'' answered Lafe. ''We got a cabin rented on the edge of town. He's lazing around and eating good. By next spring he'll be ready to climb up into the mountains with us.''

''Glad to hear that,'' Luke said.

''We saw you traded off that contrary woman that was riding with you,'' Lafe said.

''What do you mean, 'traded her off'?'' Luke felt a chill at the mention of Susan.

''Why we saw her with another man out there in the mouth of the South Platte River. Snowing it was and hard. We came up on this tall fellow with a black beard. Because of the thick snow, we didn't see him or him us until we were close. I swear, I believe the man was damn mad to run into us. He seemed about to pull a gun. However, there being four of us with our guns handy, that stopped him. He gave us a mean look, yelled at the woman and rode off in the snow.''

Coldiron's blood chured at the sudden knowledge. "How do you know it was the same woman?"

"Well, she did have a blanket over her shoulders because of the cold, but I saw her face and that same painted Indian shirt she wore that time we met out on the prairie."

"It can't be," exclaimed Luke.

"Sure it was her. I remembered her face and that black hair. My sons recognized her, too. She's kind of a pretty woman and a man wouldn't forget her quick."

"When did you see her?"

"Late yesterday about an hour before dark."

Luke stopped walking and leaned weakly against the front of a building. The Pertusset men halted and turned to watch him.

How could Susan be on the South Platte? Luke recalled the moment, seeing in his mind the person tumbling from the canyon rim. Yet his view of the figure that had fallen into the river had been from at least two hundred yards. Was he mistaken in what he thought he saw? Did a man have Susan a prisoner somewhere on the South Platte River?"

."How many horses did the man and woman have with them?" Luke asked.

"Two riding horses and three with packs. The animals were thin, as if they had been on short rations lately."

"She is alive," Luke spoke in a low, disbelieving voice. He did not understand what had happened, but somehow Susan was alive. One of the outlaws must have been the person that fell into the river. He clasped Lafe by the shoulders. "This is great news! Great news!"

"I see you have changed your opinion of the woman," grinned Pertusset.

"Some," Coldiron said. "I got to find the man and woman. I must know who they are. Tell me exactly where you met them."

"About three miles upstream above where the South Platte leaves the face of the mountains. The valley is squeezed in there until it's not over a hundred yards wide. In that narrow place we saw them coming up the trail as we came down. Passed within fifty feet of each other. With all the supplies they were packing, I'd say they could spend the winter up there."

Luke looked up at the brittle stars in the sky. The night was late. He could do nothing until the morning. He spoke to Lafe. "Could I sleep at your place for a few hours?"

"Sure. Be glad for your company. There'll be a warm fire at the cabin. You look like you are hungry. We'll cook some supper. If you want a packhorse, we might even loan you one we took recently from a fellow out on the prairie." All the Pertussets laughed.

Luke did not laugh. The feeling of anger and hate ran through his mind like ice water. He rested his hand on the butt of his six-gun. He was going to kill a man.

The Pertussets would loan him some gold. Then at first light he would buy provisions, a new skinning knife and fresh cartridges. By midafteroon the valley of the South Platte could be reached.

Somehow he knew his enemy would be there in the snowy forest of the mountains. Luke was not so sure Susan would be.

CHAPTER 18

A biting wind came off the mountains to flay Luke's face and crease it with cold. He tugged his hat down more firmly on his head and held the Indian pony to the hard pace over the snow-shrouded land.

On Luke's left the South Platte River bent its never ending flow along a meandering channel. He did not follow the long looping turns, but scouted the terrain ahead with his eyes and rode straight from the outside of one curve to the next.

The sere, frozen emptiness of the prairie was left behind, and the course traversed among the low foothills to enter the valley that had been cut through the mountains by the river during ages long past. As the route climbed into the high country, the snow grew deeper and the scrubby brush gave way to pine trees.

Luke found the man tracks of the Pertusset clan and the sign of their one packhorse. Two miles farther up the valley he located the place where the Pertussets had encountered the outlaw and his band of horses.

Coldiron stared at the tracks the animals had cut in the snow. They were familiar and he recognized them without dismounting.

Luke's breath came fast. Susan had ridden past this very spot as a captive on one of those mounts. He could feel the wolf rising in his heart, when a man would do reckless, savage things without thought of danger or consequence.

He must hurry. He struck the black, urging it onward. Luke rode the cold and did not feel it at all.

The course circled to go around a great rocky ridge. On the sharp crest of the hill, clumps of stunted pines burrowed tenacious tentacle roots into the scant soil at the base of tall spires of rock. The pines, exposed for their lifetime to the relentless push and shove of the wind, were barbered and twisted into strange, tortured forms.

In the fierce, unpredictable drafts of wind at the peak of the ridge, an old male raven and a younger one played unfriendly games of nerve and skill—rising, falling, tilting, darting dangerously among the rocky pinnacles. As Luke passed far below, he looked up at the birds pitting their skill, one against the other.

Both birds, speeding on thick black wings perilously close to the rock-studded ground, the younger in pursuit of the older, vanished behind the ridge. Luke watched for them to come into view once again and continue their foolish game. They did not reappear and he wondered if they had been dashed to their deaths.

Farther on he discovered where the bandit had made a night camp. Two sets of footprints were imprinted in the snow. One pair was considerably smaller than the other; a woman's boots could have made them.

The larger person had waded the snow up to a point of land above the camp and spent a long time where he could spy up and down the stream channel and reach every point with a rifle shot.

Luke pushed on. The evening came and the sun sank. The sky turned black and was mostly obscured by the mountains that towered on all sides. The tumultuous wind slowed its cascade down the mountain and lay quiet.

In the gloom of the nighttide the trampled path of the five horses faded and merged with the countless shadows on the snow. Luke pulled the black to a halt and swung stiffly to the ground. He squatted on his haunches and waited for the moon to come up. No thought of making camp came to him. Susan must be taken from the outlaw this night. If she was still alive.

A listening silence settled upon the land. The cold of the mountaintop, heavy with its own weight, slid down the steep hillsides to concentrate in the valley. The temperature fell swiftly.

Luke stood up and began to pace a short way back and forth. The mushy noise the snow had emitted from under the horses' hooves all day turned to a brittle, crackling sound as the ice crystals hardened with the deepening cold.

The thin horn curve of the dying moon rose in the east. With it came the beginning of a breeze from the prairie, snaking up the river channel, moaning through the leafless branches of the willows and cottonwoods on the stream bank.

The light of the moon threw an army of shadows among the trees and brought to life again the tracks of the outlaws. Coldiron mounted and continued the chase.

In the treacherous footing of a boulder patch, the snow was trampled and smashed where one of the five horses had fallen. Luke hoped fervently Susan had not been riding the animal that fell.

As he trekked upward beside the river, the snow deepened, reaching halfway to the knees of the horse. The flanks of the mountain crowded nearer. The pine trees became larger and rose up to block the moonlight. In the gloom the trail became hidden. Still, Luke pressed ahead, for the sign could not be lost in the narrow confines of the valley.

Where a tributary emptied into the South Platte, the tracks swerved to follow the smaller stream. Soon the path was forced away from the bank of the creek and up a long slope toward a high bench.

The grade steepened and Luke dismounted to continue the climb on foot. After a short way his labored breathing was mixed with that of the valiant black, huffing at his heels.

He came out onto the top of the bench. The nearly vertical flank of the mountain was a hundred paces to his right. A third that far on his other side, the bench broke away steeply down to the creek.

The winds swept up behind him, shrieking a wild song along the bench. Luke mounted the horse and leaned far over its neck to let the clawing, hurricane wind run up his back and glance away. The light, dry snow was picked up by the wind and flowed in ground streams of white across the cleft of land and into thick pine woods at the far end. Luke went warily into the forest.

Near the stump of a dead tree the snow was littered with chips of wood where someone had chopped a large supply of fuel. A well-beaten footpath in the snow led straight away.

The camp of Luke's enemy was very near. Somewhere there at the end of the path.

The wind, deflected by the tall trees, swirled in turbulent eddies. One fast puff carried woodsmoke to Luke and he stopped quickly at the smell.

He retreated back along the trail and securely fastened the horse. Taking his rifle, he slipped cautiously forward again.

Luke saw the small log cabin etched in low dark outline on the snow in a clearing of a quarter acre or so. For many minutes he surveyed the scene. He spotted the indistinct forms of several motionless horses on the far side of the structure. Nothing moved about the cabin and no light showed.

A burst of sparks shot up from the chimney, chasing smoke into the night gloom of the air. Someone had thrown wood on the fire. The outlaw was still awake.

Luke crept up to the back of the cabin and pressed close to the wall. The logs were small in diameter, as if limited to what one man could lift by himself. They were flattened somewhat with an ax for close fit. The spaces between them were chinked snugly with moss and mud. He stole along, looking for a glimmer of light through a crack so he could see into the interior.

At last, the unknown man who had robbed and killed and made Susan a prisoner had been run to ground in his lair. Now to devise a plan to destroy him.

A frontal attack to batter open the door of the stronghold could easily fail, and Susan might be injured in the gunfight. The chimney could be plugged so smoke would fill the inside and perhaps drive the man from the building. However, the man would not be fooled by that trick. But rather he would merely quench the fire. And he would be warned of the danger outside.

Better Luke quietly wait. Sooner or later the outlaw had to come out of the protective walls. A final, fatal error had been made by the man.

Luke moved around the corner of the cabin to go to a vantage point from which to watch the front and make his attack. A sudden chilling premonition of danger tightened his scalp. With a long, swift step backward, he pulled behind the cabin. His adversary had made not one faulty judgment in all the days Luke had hunted him. Why would he now go into a small cabin and let his enemies gather to fire upon him from the safety of the woods?

Luke knew with certainty the outlaw would not be so senseless. At the camp the night before on the main stem of the river, the man had taken a defensive position and maintained it for hours. He would do the same here, guarding each hour, day and night, until heavy snow concealed his winter bivouac from all those who would harm him.

Luke cast a searching look about through the forest. The man was out there, primed and biding his time.

But where? If he had been defending the trail, Luke would have been dead by now. No, he had to be at a place where he could spot an opponent approaching the door of the cabin and at the same time see that Susan did not escape.

Luke hunched low and went straight away from the building and into the forest. From tree to tree he stalked, circling, moving only when the wind made noises in the tops of the trees where the black limbs scratched at the black sky.

Through a break in the woods he saw a front corner of the cabin. He altered his course. The trees became more dense. The canopies overhead merged to block out the moonlight and hide the forest in murk.

A short distance further the forest thinned and an avenue lay open to the full front of the cabin. The moon shined down unhindered among the sparse trees. Every object was sharply silhouetted, framed against the snow made luminous by the moonlight.

The outlaw would be here, and he had simply to wait for Luke to come within the range of his gun or the reach of his knife.

The wind, slowed by the trees, was in Luke's face. He raised his head, as does a hunting animal, and breathed of the black air. It was drawn slowly past the sensitive nerve endings of his nostrils. The scent of pine needles, pitch and old bark. The cold, damp odor of snow.

He moved one silent step at a time in the direction of the forest at the end of the clearing. He smelled the granite rock of the mountain and moldy wood.

More steps, and the odor of tanned buffalo hide reached Luke. So very familiar, after his having slept uncounted nights rolled up in such a covering.

He tested again. The sour smell of an unwashed human body rode the air.

Luke's unknown foe was directly upwind.

Holding the scent, Luke crept among the trees. The outlaw would be within a few yards at most.

The figure of a man wrapped in a heavy covering and wearing a hat became visible sitting at the base of a large tree with low-growing limbs. Coldiron lifted his rifle and sighted along the barrel.

Something was wrong. The figure was too still. Luke lowered his weapon. To shoot at a false target would give away all surprise.

Luke removed the leather thong from the hammer of his six-gun. Then he crept forward, drawing as close as he dared. With a rush, he sprang upon the seated form.

His knife stabbed deeply. He expected to feel the keen edge cutting into a solid body. He felt only the wool of a blanket, and the figure collapsed without substance beneath him.

Luke's cunning foe had set a trap. Pine branches had been encased in the blanket. Luke flung himself to roll away in the slippery snow.

A man plummeted down from the limbs of the tree overhead. The crushing feet glanced off Luke's spinning body. A knife slashed to cut a long slice through Luke's coat at the shoulder. He sensed the blade severing his flesh, but there was no pain.

Clason sprang after Luke and cut at him again. Luke stopped his roll and caught the knife arm of his opponent. The sharp point of steel embedded itself in Luke's wrist before he could force it to a halt. He thrust up with his own weapon.

Clason faded to the side, and the knife skittered a glancing cut across his ribs, laying the muscle and tendons open for several inches. Before Luke could withdraw his hand, Clason caught a vise-like hold on it. Instantly, one of his hard boots lashed out, smashing into Luke's chest.

Coldiron thought his ribs were shattered. He jerked the

man down on the snowy ground beside him and kicked out fiercely with his feet. They landed solidly in Clason's stomach. Quickly, before the outlaw could shelter himself, Coldiron kicked him once more.

Severely damaged by the blows and knife cuts, the two men recoiled from each other and leaped to their feet. Breathing painfully and favoring their wounds, they faced each other. In the gloom beneath the tree they planted their feet in the snow and held their knives poised to strike.

Coldiron leaned toward the outlaw, searching for an opportunity to attack, and prepared to counterattack. The man was strong, very strong, and amazingly quick. They were closely matched. Because of that, the two of them might injure each other so badly both would die.

Clason laughed three guttural notes. "There's a quicker way to end this," he said.

"Yes," agreed Luke, and took his knife in his left hand. Would his six-gun be in the holster and in the proper position for a fast draw after being wallowed in the snow? Would it fire?

Clason chuckled again and shifted his long blade from his gun hand. "Let Satan take the unlucky one." His hand dipped for his pistol.

Luke reached for his six-gun. The snowy tail of his coat was flipped out of the way. The butt of the weapon stroked his palm. A comforting feeling. His finger went into the trigger guard and the thumb to the hammer.

With a flick of his wrist, he drew the gun. As it came level and half extended, he fired.

A red flame exploded from the end of the barrel, driving the lead projectile in front of it. The lance of burning powder elongated, extending across the murky distance separating Coldiron from Clason. It touched the center of the outlaw's chest, and just for a moment held there, bridging the gap, binding the two men together with its fiery tendril.

The slam of the bullet drove Clason stumbling backward. He slipped on the snow, his feet suddenly clumsy. He dropped his six-gun and fell.

Luke went to the man and knelt over him. He struck a flame on the end of a match and cupped it in his hand to shine on the outlaw's face.

Clason's glassy eyes glared up from deep sockets at Coldiron. His chest heaved and a bubbly sound came from his throat.

Neither man spoke, each watching the face of the other. The match burned down to Luke's fingertips and he let it fall to the snow.

In the darkness a shuddering breath came from Clason. Then all was very still.

Luke lifted the limp body of the outlaw over his shoulder and walked off through the woods. At the end of the high bank above the creek, he halted, hoisted the lanky form above his head and heaved mightily. The body disappeared into the blackness of the valley below.

"No burial for you," Coldiron said into the night.

Luke knocked on the door of the cabin. "Susan," he called.

"Luke! Is that you, Luke?" The door was jerked open and Susan stood holding a length of wood as a club in her hands. She dropped the makeshift weapon and stepped toward Luke.

"I heard the shot and was so very worried." She hesitated for a small fragment of time. "Are we all alone?"

"Yes. We are all alone."

"You are bleeding. Come in and let me help you." She reached out and took him by the hand and drew him inside.

The warm pressure of her hand thrilled Luke and her tanned face glowed with happiness in the light from the fireplace. She was grand to look upon.

He caught the fine, firm jaw between his fingers and tenderly held it. "Just stand very still for a few minutes and let me look at you," he said.

"And then we will talk," she replied.

ABOUT THE AUTHOR

F.M. Parker has worked as a sheepherder, lumberman, sailor, geologist, and as a manager of wild horses, buffalo, and livestock grazing. He currently manages five million acres of rangeland in eastern Oregon. He is also the author of three other Signet Brand Westerns, *The Searchers, Coldiron,* and *Skinner.* Mr. Parker lives in Vale, Oregon.